Maybe Never, Maybe Now

Sequel to the award-winning novel, *Painting Caitlyn

"... a realistic and powerful picture of how subtle and confusing abuse in its different forms can be." – *KLIATT**

"... more than just a simple problem novel. The characters are drawn with real complexity ..." – *Booklist**

"Peters clearly has her finger on the pulse of teenage dating ..." – *School Library Journal**

Maybe Never, Maybe Now
Text © 2010 Kimberly Joy Peters

Published by Lobster Press™
1620 Sherbrooke Street West, Suites C & D
Montréal, Québec H3H 1C9
Tel. (514) 904-1100 • Fax (514) 904-1101 • www.lobsterpress.com

Publisher: Alison Fripp
Editorial Directors: Meghan Nolan & Mahak Jain
Editor: Shiran Teitelbaum
Editorial Assistants: Katherine Mason & Stephanie Campbell
Graphic Design & Production: Tammy Desnoyers

 Canadian Heritage Patrimoine canadien   We acknowledge the financial support of the Government of Canada through the Canada Book Fund for our publishing activities..

Library and Archives Canada Cataloguing in Publication

Peters, Kimberly Joy, 1969-
    Maybe never, maybe now / Kimberly Joy Peters.

Sequel to: Painting Caitlyn.
ISBN 978-1-897550-64-9

    I. Title.

PS8631.E823M39 2010   jC813'.6   C2009-905722-0

Formica is a trademark of Formica Co.; **Google** is a trademark of Google Inc.; **Styrofoam** is a trademark of The Dow Chemical Company; **Ouija** is a trademark of Hasbro Inc.

Printed and bound in Canada.

    Text is printed on 100% recycled post-consumer fibre.

For my mom, with love.

– Kimberly Joy Peters

Maybe Never, Maybe Now

written by
Kimberly Joy Peters

Lobster Press ™

Chapter 1

Sometimes I wonder whether things would have been easier if I'd had a crystal ball. I might have foreseen, then, how everything that happened before would ultimately affect everything that happened after.

I also might have recognized that second chances are so much more fragile than firsts. Because even if you're lucky enough to get a second chance, you already understand how badly things can turn out. You start to realize how much more it's going to hurt if everything somehow goes wrong again. And if you don't believe, deep down, that you really deserve that second chance, the very idea of one can be paralyzing.

That's what happened to me the year I turned sixteen.

* * *

I knew the eleventh grade was going to be very different from the tenth. My two best friends, Ashley and Conner, were going on a French-language exchange in Quebec, and leaving me behind. I planned to keep busy painting scenery for the school's production of *Camelot*.

Ashley had been anticipating the exchange ever since we'd started high school, and had applied at the end of tenth grade. At the time, I'd completely dismissed the suggestion that I join her. I was an emotional mess, and in no shape to go anywhere.

For one thing, I'd recently made the switch from only child to big sister – not an easy adjustment at fifteen, however much I adored my mom and stepdad's new baby. My baby sister was only a couple of months old when applications went out for the exchange program, and my family and I were still adjusting to the new addition. I couldn't just take off before even getting to know her.

I'd also just ended an abusive relationship with my first real boyfriend, Tyler. He'd seemed perfect, in the beginning. But little by little, he'd picked away at my self-esteem, until I doubted myself so much that even when he started hitting me, I didn't tell anyone or dump him. It wasn't until he finally did it in front of my friends that I had to stop pretending everything was okay.

And while it was the physical abuse that horrified my family and friends the most, the real damage, for me, was emotional. Even though I learned later that the abuse wasn't my fault, discovering that I'd misjudged Tyler made me question every major life decision I'd ever made. I was in counseling when the exchange applications were submitted, but I still couldn't envision myself six months down the road, happy again, ready to travel, deal with a new language, and meet new people.

Months later, my own problems seemed almost insignificant compared to the challenges Ashley was facing. Her mom had breast cancer. At first, her doctors said she would just need surgery and a bit of radiation. But the cancer was proving to be more stubborn than they'd anticipated, and Ashley's mom started chemotherapy the same day we began eleventh grade.

"I just don't know how my mom's going to react to her treatments," Ashley said matter-of-factly at lunch. Her tone didn't reflect any great concern, but I knew her well enough to recognize that even talking about it was extremely difficult for her. Keeping cool on the outside was her way of trying to settle her insides – something she'd picked up from her mom.

"And," she continued, keeping her eyes focused on her lunch, "of course my mom doesn't want her illness to dictate my life. But we're all kind of in limbo right now. Which becomes a bigger problem, because the exchange is reciprocal – my partner is supposed to stay with us next semester. I mean, I can't have some girl move in if my mom is sick. As much as I hate to do it, I need to back out of the trip." When she finished, she looked up, but she couldn't hold my gaze.

I knew her well enough to realize that she wouldn't want to get much deeper into her feelings about her mom and her disappointment about not going on the trip in the middle of a crowded cafeteria. I tried to keep the discussion as emotionally neutral as she had.

"Have you already talked to Madame Galipeau?" I asked, wondering how the French teacher had reacted.

"Madame Galipeau was pretty good about it. She

said she was going to let the other school know that they'd have to make other arrangements for Mireille, my exchange partner."

Ashley talked a bit more about her partner (whose name sounded like *Meer-ay*), with whom she was supposed to live and practice her French. I knew by the way Ashley shook her head as she spoke that she felt guilty about ruining Mireille's plans too.

"It's supposed to be such a great program," she continued, finally looking at me straight on. "Which is why I think *you* should go in my place."

My mouth fell open. Despite having already suspected that Ashley might have to consider canceling her exchange, it hadn't occurred to me that her change of plans could lead to my second chance. And although I was usually a bit more flexible than Ashley, I wasn't one to act super-impulsively.

"I don't know," I said, completely lost for words. It wasn't just that I was afraid of dealing with the unknown. I was also thinking that I could offer more emotional support to Ashley if I stayed home.

Still, French was an easy subject for me, and all of my

earlier reasons for staying home suddenly seemed stupid. So, while I teetered between wanting to take a chance and feeling I should stay home, Ashley explained that if I did decide to go, I'd get all of my credits and come back speaking fluent French.

"Quebec is supposed to be breathtakingly beautiful," she said, looking at me with the gorgeous smile that had led her into professional modeling.

I sighed, thinking about how much I didn't want to abandon her when her boyfriend had just dumped her and her mom was so sick. "It would be so much better if we could *both* go," I insisted.

"You won't miss me as much as you expect, because you'll be there with Conner," she reminded me with a half smile.

I didn't admit it to Ashley, but I didn't need any reminders that Conner had also signed up to go. Conner and I had been friends for years, and we'd worked together doing arts and crafts at a daycare all summer. He'd spoken at length about the exchange, while I quietly cursed myself for not having signed up. I had wondered what I would do with both my best friends gone for an entire semester.

I knew I shouldn't factor Conner into my decision. Still, knowing that he'd be there was reassuring. Knowing that Ashley *wouldn't* be there made me ache for her. She'd been incredibly strong throughout her mother's illness. Her own big breakup, after two years, had been completely unexpected. We all thought she and her boyfriend would be the kind of high school sweethearts who stay together forever, even though they were quite young when they started dating. Missing out on the exchange was one more sucky thing she would have to deal with. I felt like a traitor as I considered leaving her behind.

"I wouldn't go to be with Conner," I told her. "But I would stay for you, if you want me to. You have so much going on right now."

"No," she shook her head. "Don't even consider that. If you don't want to do it, that's one thing. But if you have even the tiniest desire to go, I think you should. Don't you want to be able to study art in Paris someday?"

"Hopefully ..." I acknowledged.

"Then go to Quebec this semester, and learn the language."

That's what I loved about Ashley. She didn't see problems – she saw solutions. And she had the confidence that I'd always lacked.

"Can you come over and convince my mom?" I laughed as I hugged her. "You're so much better at it than I'll ever be!"

And my prediction came true: Mom required a huge sales pitch. She'd been a single parent until I was seven. Then, she married my stepdad, Mike. I think that made her relax a little bit, because all of a sudden she had "backup" when it came to making decisions for me. The year before, though, she'd been distracted by her pregnancy. For the first time, she'd let her guard down just as I started dating Tyler. And no matter what I said to the contrary, she still felt like some of the stuff that had happened with him was her fault. Even though I was about to turn sixteen, she was reluctant to send me off to a province where English wasn't even the primary language.

"I don't know," she said, shaking her head and looking at my stepdad for advice. "I'm just not really comfortable having you so far away."

Translation: she didn't trust me. And after the way I'd

snuck around behind her back with Tyler the year before (I still had the belly ring to remind us all), I didn't really blame her. But that didn't stop me from wanting to go.

"You've always said a second language is really important," I reminded her. "You know, to make me more well-rounded."

"Well, yes, the language opportunity is excellent. But I'm also concerned about your other subjects. You have to start looking at colleges soon, and I don't want you to end up struggling academically this year because of a language barrier in your classes."

As opposed to the way I'd messed up my academics the year before, because of Tyler, I thought to myself.

"They must make some provisions for that," Mike stepped in. A year ago, I might have seen his interest in me going on an exchange as an excuse to get me out of the house. But we'd gotten much closer over the past few months, and I appreciated his support. I shot him a grateful smile.

"Ashley says I should just arrange my schedule so I can take my lighter subjects while in Quebec," I assured them. "Besides, I have my free period this semester. I'll have to take French, of course, but I'll be in it with all the other exchange students. And I can totally handle bilingual gym and art," I added.

"Won't that make for a really heavy second semester when you get home?" Mom asked doubtfully.

I decided to switch tactics. "Please? It'll be like a whole fresh start for me."

"I think we should let her do it." Mike put his arms around Mom, and I knew I'd won.

"But Angelique is growing up so fast – Caitlyn will miss so much if she goes away," she protested, glancing over at my little sister, now seven months old.

"Caitlyn's growing up fast too. And she needs this opportunity to test her independence a little bit before she goes off to college – at which point, she'll also have to miss out on her little sister's day-to-day development. We can't keep her home forever."

Mom made one last feeble attempt at protest: "What about your goldfish? You can't take it to Quebec."

"I'll take care of Goldie," Mike said. "And you," he said to my mother, "will be fine too."

* * *

By the third day back to school, I'd settled everything.

"*Fantastique*," Ashley said during lunch, after I'd explained to her that I was officially signed up and that my schedule had been adjusted. Conner had even given me a brand new French/English dictionary to celebrate my joining the exchange. I had also talked Ashley into trying out for the school musical, ensuring that she, too, would be doing something new and fabulous while I was away, despite her mother's health.

"But you know you still have some big decisions to make, right?" she asked one day, smiling.

I panicked, trying to figure out what I might have forgotten. "What decisions?"

"Like, how you want to celebrate your sixteenth birthday before you go."

Dumb as it sounds, I think I flinched a little bit at the mention of a birthday. It wasn't the birthday that was the problem. Just the idea of celebrating it.

Chapter 2

Tyler and I had been going out for a while before my fifteenth birthday. And he'd gone to a lot of trouble to make it really special. Not only did he create an elaborate treasure hunt on the beach and register a star in my name, he also bought me Goldie, my goldfish. It had been just the two of us that night, enjoying each other's company.

But in the end, the relationship got so twisted and ended so horribly that even the good memories, like my birthday, felt tainted.

So I didn't want to do anything too planned this year. And I'd been to enough Sweet Sixteen parties to know that having a big bash probably wasn't a good option for me either. Besides, I could never pull off the kind of drunken parties a lot of people arranged when their parents left town, and I wouldn't have wanted to anyway.

I decided instead to spend my birthday with my family, since Mom was feeling so anxious about my going away. I hoped it would reassure her that no matter what, she was still an important part of my life.

Besides, when I really considered it, Ashley and Conner were the two people who had supported me the most during the previous year. But Conner would be with me in Quebec – Ashley wouldn't.

I felt bad enough that Ashley was giving up her trip for my benefit. I didn't want to make a big deal about a party too. In the end, I suggested that we just spend the day together, celebrating in a non-birthday kind of way. We decided to go to the Fall Fair.

I'd been there before with Tyler, but not on my birthday. He'd entered some of my artwork – without my knowledge – into the art competition there. And as badly as our relationship turned out, that had been a good night for us too. Without his initiative, I never would have had the confidence to enter anything on my own.

Now, reassured by a few art competitions that I'd entered *myself*, I was determined not to let Tyler's shadow cloud my day with Ashley. I would do whatever I could to spend one last memorable Saturday with her before I left.

Although she wouldn't admit that anything was wrong, Ashley seemed really quiet, as if she had her own dark cloud hanging above her. She tried to chalk it up to not sleeping well. When she skipped her favorite fix of cotton candy, though, I knew she wasn't feeling like herself, and I worried again about going away. My best friend had so many crappy things happening in her life. This day wasn't supposed to be just about me – I wanted to make it fun for her too. Which was why I got so excited when I saw the fortune-teller's wagon, painted with the words "*Madame Syeira Sees All!*"

At first, Ashley did her whole "practical" thing on me, stating that if Madame Syeira was the real deal, she'd already be rich from the stock markets or something. I tried my best to persuade her. I suggested that maybe reading people was different from analyzing stock markets. When that didn't convince her, I appealed to her curiosity.

"You've heard of the artist Salvador Dali, right?" I asked. Not waiting for a response, I continued. "He was a surrealist painter. And he designed a whole deck of tarot cards that was released the year he turned eighty. Maybe she has one of those sets. I'd love to see them. And anyway," I said, "that sign says there's a discount if you get two readings, so I think we should both go."

Ashley offered to pay for two readings for me, as a birthday gift, but I refused. I knew she had more of a rational mind than me, which sometimes made it harder for her to open herself to the unconventional. But I wasn't going to let her off the hook that easily.

"Nope," I told her. "We're both going."

It wasn't that I totally believed in fortune-telling either. It was just that it felt like I was finally waking up from the bad dream that had been Tyler, and I wanted to hear that good things were coming my way. Even if the person saying them was paid to do so. I thought that with everything going on in her life, Ashley could benefit from the same.

Reluctantly, she agreed and stepped into the trailer. I went first and followed a beautifully dressed woman, who called herself Madame Syeira, through a beaded curtain, into a room decorated with heavy furnishings and jewel-toned colors.

"How may I help you?" she asked from across the

small table where she'd seated me.

Since I didn't really believe in this stuff, I wasn't sure that it would make a difference what type of "fortune-telling" I asked for. When she told me she didn't have the Dali tarot cards, I settled for a palm reading instead.

She nodded, as if she'd known that was what I would say, and held her hands out across the tablecloth to indicate that I should give her mine. "You relax, and I'll see what your palm says."

As instructed, I turned my hand over to her, and studied her face while she studied my palm. Her expression was one of intense concentration, which made me wonder whether she actually saw something interesting, or was just working really hard to persuade me that she did.

"I see many tears," she said, and I felt my hand twitch. I had cried so much over Tyler, and the things he'd done to me. I almost cried again, from relief, when she said, "But many of the tears are now tears of happiness. Your family is very important to you, but you have missed out on much time with a loved one. You are very creative, but often unsure of yourself, and reluctant to take chances. And you have a trip in your future, a long trip somewhere far. You will travel much in your lifetime, and this will bring great happiness."

Although it was all more or less accurate, I was embarrassed that she somehow knew I was often unsure of myself and reluctant to take chances. For a moment, I was tempted to point out that I *was* stepping outside my comfort zone by taking a trip. But the fact that I didn't proved even more that traveling wasn't my only source of uncertainty.

"What about my love line?" I asked, wanting to see what she would come up with. She squinted a bit, and then traced it with her long fingernail. "It begins weakly, thin, a bit broken," she said, showing me the place between my thumb and index finger. "There's some heartache. You were very emotional. But here," she moved further along, "here it is stronger, deeper, and continuous. There is great love in your future."

I knew I wasn't ready for "great love" yet. But I liked knowing that it would be there for me someday.

Like it or not, she'd been really accurate in the way she described me. I'd gone in with a healthy skepticism, but I left a believer. While Ashley went in for her own reading,

I wrote down everything I could remember from mine.

Unfortunately, Ashley's experience wasn't nearly as positive.

"First, like a total klutz, I knocked all the tarot cards onto the floor," she explained afterward. "I think she just felt me tense up ..."

By that point, Ashley had been even more convinced that the whole thing was fixed, that Madame Syeira was just reading our body language and had sensed that Ashley just wasn't into it. Madame Syeira ended up telling Ashley that her energies weren't in a good place for a proper reading, and gave her a mood ring instead. I was admiring it, and actually thinking about going back to buy one for myself, when Ashley held it out to me and told me to try it on.

In seconds, like the dark of night changing into a beautiful sunny day, the ring went from black to a bright turquoise. The color chart that came with it said that a dark stone, as it had been while Ashley wore it, indicated stress and tension. Which made perfect sense considering how sick her mom was and her recent breakup with Brandon. But turquoise meant I was in a calm, relaxed mood.

When Ashley told me to keep it, I spun it around my finger a few times to see if it had a different color for guilt. Guilt that I was going on the trip in the first place. Guilt that she was tense and I wasn't. Guilt that I'd really wanted the ring and, somehow, she'd picked up on that enough to offer it to me.

While I stood there feeling torn up inside, she told me about some of the meditation and alternative treatments she wanted her mother to try. She'd been reading up on some theory that said stress actually might have caused her mother's cancer. She wanted her mom to try relaxation training, which was supposed to help her mother get better. I loved Ashley, but I couldn't believe she could be so dismissive of palm readings, and yet so interested in a theory that blamed her mother for a disease that people had little control over.

"I don't think that's fair," I said. "It's like when I thought that if I were a better girlfriend, Tyler would treat me better. But I didn't cause his anger issues. And I don't think your mom's stress caused her cancer."

"Maybe not," she said. That, at least, was progress. So I backed off, remembering how unselfish she was to be sending me off on the trip of a lifetime while she stayed home.

Several onion rings and hours of fun later, we parted. And I knew it was kind of crazy, but every time I looked down at my mood ring that afternoon, I felt better about the exchange. It was as if the turquoise glow of the ring confirmed that going was the right thing to do.

But as the bus pulled away from the school on Monday morning, and I waved back at my family and my best friend, I wondered again if it really was.

Chapter 3

Conner had saved me a seat on the bus that would take us to the train station. From there, we had a seventeen-hour trip that would lead us to a tiny town on the southern shores of the Saint Lawrence River.

I sighed deeply as I lost sight of Ashley.

"She'll be okay," Conner said reassuringly, as if he'd read my mind.

"I know ... it's just that Ashley was really looking forward to this trip. She should be sitting here – not me."

"*She* can't. But I'm glad *you're* here," he said, squeezing my hand. The heat from his fingers made my ring change from turquoise to green. I noticed that it was the same color as his eyes, which were partially covered by his plum-colored bangs.

I was glad he was there too. At one time, Conner and

I had just been classmates. We'd sit together and make small talk during art class, but that was it. Then, we'd been recruited by one of our art teachers to do a mural. After spending so much time together, I'd grown to appreciate his creativity and personal insight. His outward appearance tended to be a bit wild, with dyed hair and multiple piercings, but he had a way of making me feel completely relaxed and comfortable.

Then during the whole Tyler-era, I'd pulled away from Conner. Partly it was because Tyler had been jealous of our friendship. But I also distanced myself because Conner had asked me a lot of good questions that had difficult answers I felt uncomfortable thinking about. Like, did I love Tyler or just the idea of him? And why didn't I seem happy if things were truly as good as I claimed? And, most pointedly of all, did going out with Tyler make me a better person?

At the time, I hadn't even been able to answer most of those questions for myself, let alone talk about them with someone else. And so, it had felt easier to just avoid the questions – and the answers I didn't want to face – by avoiding Conner too.

Still, like Ashley, Conner never gave up on me. And after the breakup, he recommended me for a summer job where I worked with him at an arts and crafts camp. I wouldn't have taken the job if Conner hadn't pushed me, which, it occurred to me now, was probably what Madame Syeira had meant about me being reluctant to take chances.

As Conner and I had started doing things together outside of school, Ashley, kidding at first, started referring to him as my "un-boyfriend." "You do everything together except boyfriend/girlfriend stuff," she said, exasperated because he was great boyfriend material, and she thought I should scoop him up before someone else did.

The thing was, I didn't want to "scoop him up." I was content – happy, even – with the way things were between us. It wasn't that I didn't find him attractive, or that I thought he was going to change and become abusive, the way Tyler had. It was, crazy as it sounds, because I liked him so much. And I'd already learned the hard way a thing that Ashley had said to me years before: "Boyfriends may come and go, but good friends are forever."

* * *

Altogether, there were twelve students – nine girls and three guys – going to Quebec from our school. We'd each been paired with a Quebecois student with whom we would live until Christmas. During our exchange, we were expected to speak French, all French, and nothing but French, so help us. Of course, the organizers weren't completely naive, and recognized that we did need to communicate with our parents and friends back home. But in the spirit of total language immersion, we'd been asked to limit our texting and e-mailing to just a couple of times a week.

The twelve of us sat together on the train and talked about what we expected from the exchange. Some of us were going for the opportunity to learn the language, experience a new culture, and escape the lives we'd been leading. Others just thought it would be fun to party for a couple of months. But whatever our reasons, I noticed that everyone looked a little bit panicky as we finally pulled into a tiny train station in the middle of the night.

Despite the late hour, about thirty people were waiting at the platform to greet us. They held up homemade signs with our names on them to help us identify our host families. Conner found his exchange partner, Alexandre, right away.

"*Bonsoir! Je m'appelle Conner,*" I heard him introduce himself to his new host family with a confidence I envied. I looked around, trying to find Mireille. Conner carried his guitar over his shoulder, holding onto its case while dragging three bags behind him in his other hand. I'd already teased him about women being the ones who were supposed to pack too much, but now I was thinking that it would have been reassuring to have more of my own things with me.

I wished I could have found Mireille as easily as Conner had found Alexandre. Doing my best not to look pathetic as I searched for her, I dragged my own luggage behind me. Finally, I spotted a small blond girl holding a sign with my name on it, standing on her tiptoes to see above the crowd. "See you tomorrow," I said, brushing past Conner as I approached her, hating the way everything familiar had suddenly slipped away. I pushed through the crowds to Mireille and introduced myself.

"*Bonsoir. Je m'appelle Caitlyn,*" I said.

"*Caitlyn!*" she jumped up and down and enveloped

me in a hug. I thought I heard her introduce her parents to me as Sylvie and Gilbert, but I wasn't positive, because she spoke very quickly. And although her words sounded like French, her accent was utterly different from what I'd learned at school. I had to focus on every word. Two smaller children, a boy and a girl, hid shyly behind her parents. I knew, from what Madame Galipeau had told me, that Mireille had four siblings. But in all the noise and chaos, I missed hearing the names of the little ones. My mouth went dry, and I couldn't make it work to ask again.

Somehow, I managed to hand over most of my bags to Mireille's family. Mireille took one of them and we followed her family back to their van. The drive from the station to their home couldn't have taken more than five minutes, but it felt like hours as I attempted to translate every sentence they spoke, seeking familiar words and patterns. The little ones were warming up, shrieking and giggling. But by the time Gilbert pulled into the driveway and cut the ignition, I knew I was going to like them all. Everyone seemed to smile and make each other laugh a lot. Still, I was beginning to feel that in all my years of language classes, I'd never been taught a single useful thing.

Sylvie invited me into a large kitchen with Mireille while Gilbert hustled the little ones off to bed. She spoke to me in a nasal accent.

"Veux-tu un toast?" By the way her voice and her eyebrows rose at the end of the phrase, it was easy to see that she was asking me a question.

"Un toast?"

I searched my memory, thinking back quickly over every word I'd ever learned in French class, trying to remember what *toast* meant. And though I was trying to stay calm, my confusion must have been evident. Sylvie reached for a loaf of bread, and pointed at the toaster. *"Du pain? Cuite?"* It was the same word in both languages. She was just asking me if I wanted toast.

I relaxed, and laughed at myself for making everything seem more complicated than it needed to be.

When I caught my breath, I managed a weak, *"Non, merci,"* along with a phrase that I hoped meant, "I'm happy to be here, but please speak a little more slowly." The message seemed to get through, because Mireille took my hand and said that she was also *contente* to have me there. Then, she led me upstairs to the second floor room

I'd be sharing with her.

It was a small room, with two single beds, two dressers, and two small windows dressed in white lace curtains. Mireille carried one of my bags across the room and set it down while she flopped down on the bed by the door.

It was late, and I should have been exhausted, but Mireille was obviously just as wide-awake and anxious to talk as I was. We asked each other a lot of questions, and Mireille made sure to craft her answers simply and slowly.

And so, through the early hours before dawn, I learned that Mireille loved music, chocolate, and the color purple. She played percussion in the school band. Her best friend was also her oldest sister, Marie-Claire. The younger ones were Madeleine and Sébastien, and she had another brother named Nicolas. She was so pretty and dynamic that I was surprised to discover that she didn't have a *chum* – a boyfriend. But we obviously shared similar taste in guys, as she did like a lot of my favorite actors and male musicians.

There were many times when I needed her to repeat things she'd said, and vice versa, but I did manage to tell her that I had only one sister, who was less than a year old, that I didn't have a boyfriend, and that I lived with my mom and stepfather. The part where she got confused was when I tried to explain that even though I had a stepfather, my biological father wasn't dead. At the time, I assumed that her confusion was the result of the language barrier. It wasn't until later that I realized that Mireille – a girl from a huge, loving family – just couldn't understand how my own father could drop out of my life when I was four and never try to contact me again.

And, truth be told, I didn't understand it myself.

Chapter 4

Not only did I not know my biological father, but I also spent fifteen years of my life as an only child. So waking up to Mireille's large family was almost more of a cultural shock than the language.

The day began early, and I awoke with that confused feeling you get when you're first coming out of a sound sleep and you can't quite remember where you are. As I became more conscious, I realized that Mireille was no longer in her bed, but someone was pounding on our door. Judging by the chattering, I guessed that it was Mireille's younger brother and sister. When ignoring them didn't make it stop, I stumbled over my suitcase to open the door.

"*Sal-oooo!*" her little sister shouted, grinning up at me from a mess of dark curls.

"*Salut*, Madeleine," I responded, holding up one hand to give her a high-five. The kids Conner and I had taught at craft camp during the summer had been really big on high-fives, and Madeleine seemed to be too.

Her brother, Sébastien, made karate-chopping motions, pretending to ignore me but glancing between moves to make sure I'd seen them.

They were cute, but I was exhausted. Madeleine began babbling so quickly that I couldn't understand a thing she said. While these two adorable little kids were obviously delighted to have me there, the fact that I couldn't understand them was intimidating. I stretched my arms up, hoping that if I could shake off the sleepiness, I might better understand them and get to know them more.

But as I yawned and stretched, my T-shirt slid up, and I accidentally exposed my belly ring. Madeleine's eyes sprang open while her mouth clamped shut. I didn't know what had happened until she tore off down the hall crying "*Un bijou! Maman! Elle a un bijou comme je veux!*"

The piercing had been a mistake. Tyler had pressured me into having it done without my mom's permission. It's hard to believe that I'd actually thought I could have kept it hidden from my mother. I mean, I'd just accidentally flashed it at two little kids and it wasn't even eight o'clock in the morning yet. When I'd first had it done, though, I convinced myself that I could keep it my own little secret. I used to be very good at convincing myself of stuff like that.

Anyway, it got horribly infected within a week, and I ended up really sick and totally grounded. Now, when I looked at it, a part of me still felt ashamed by my stupidity and by the way I'd allowed myself to be manipulated. I *never* intentionally showed it to anyone. But still, I couldn't quite bring myself to remove it.

Downstairs, I could hear Madeleine chattering away, and Sylvie interjecting occasionally. I couldn't make out what they were saying, though, so I didn't know whether Madeleine had admired my belly ring or been scared off by it.

We weren't expected to attend school that first morning because of our late arrival the night before. But it was becoming clear from the various sounds in the house that I wasn't going to be sleeping in either.

There was still no sign of Mireille, but her family had told me to make myself at home, so I grabbed what I needed for a shower and went down the hall to the bathroom. The door was open, and Mireille stood at the sink brushing her teeth, while an older girl – her hair wrapped in a towel – applied makeup in the mirror over the vanity.

"*Salut mon amie!*" Mireille greeted me with a mouthful of toothpaste. She spat into the sink, rinsed the brush under some water, and patted the other girl's shoulder with her free hand. "*C'est ma soeur aînée, Marie-Claire.*"

Marie-Claire was her eighteen-year-old sister. She'd already finished high school, and was taking a year off to work at the local pharmacy before deciding where to go to college.

"*Salut!*" said Marie-Claire, moving over a bit to make room for me as she said something else that I couldn't understand. I asked her to repeat herself.

Mercifully, she switched to English. "Don't be shy – come in!" she said, with a flip of her head to indicate that I should join the two of them in front of the mirror.

Making myself at home was going to be one thing.

Showering in a bathroom with an open door and two strangers was quite another. I wasn't sure whether Marie-Claire had been serious or not, but Mireille clearly saw the panic on my face. She laughed, and pushed her sister toward the door. *"Notre nouvelle soeur ne doit pas partager avec nous!"* I was relieved to learn that I didn't actually have to share the bathroom with them, and touched that Mireille had called me their new sister.

The warm water woke me up, and the few moments of quiet in the shower felt both familiar and calming. Mireille was nice. Her family was welcoming. I could handle the language thing. But on my way back down the hall after I'd showered, I caught just enough of the conversation downstairs to understand that four-year-old Madeleine was begging for a belly ring, and Sylvie had been disgusted to hear about mine.

I was trembling by the time I got back to our room.

Mireille had obviously heard the conversation, and looked at me wide-eyed when she saw me. "Madeleine says you have a belly ring," she said in French, pointing at her own stomach for emphasis. *"Elle est tellement jalouse."*

I couldn't tell from her expression whether she

admired it, as her younger sister did, or considered it "*obscène*," like her mother, so I pretended to misunderstand and instead told her the story behind my mood ring.

It looked dark and cloudy when I picked it up off the nightstand, but after a moment in my hands, it began to lighten. After trying to explain how it worked, I handed it over to Mireille. She bounced with excitement as her finger turned the ring bright orange.

"*Je l'adore!*" she shrieked, and although I loved the ring too, Ashley had been completely unselfish about giving it to me. I thought about an old saying my mother used to repeat: "Find a penny, pick it up, and all the day, you'll have good luck. Give it to a friend, and your luck will never end." Mireille's mother probably already thought I was going to be a bad influence on her daughters, and Mireille herself seemed to feel sorry for me because I didn't know my real father. New sister or not, if I was going to fit in, I definitely needed some luck. So, without a moment's hesitation, I gave the ring to Mireille.

"*Oh! Merci mille fois!*" she said, hugging me, and then switched to English. "Thank you, sister."

It was beautiful on her small finger, but for just a

moment, I wished I could try it on again to see if it would brighten up for me. It would let me know if giving it away had been the right thing to do.

Gilbert had already left for work, and Nicolas, the brother I hadn't yet met, had gone to school. Still, what Sylvie described as a "small" breakfast included six of us altogether. We ate fluffy pancakes with real maple syrup, some of which stuck to Sébastien's cheeks. Sylvie made polite conversation about the weather (it was going to be sunny) and school (she would drive us in for the afternoon). She didn't mention the belly ring – or her argument with Madeleine – but she did raise her eyebrows when Mireille showed her the mood ring, and commented tersely that I must like jewelry.

"*As-tu un autre?*" Madeleine asked with trembling lips, and I wished, because she was so cute, that I *did* have another for her. I thought quickly, and stood up to bring her the dragonfly hairclip that I had in my luggage.

All eyes went first to me, then to Mireille, as I rose. Quietly, she explained that in their family, nobody left the table until everyone had finished.

"*Désolée,*" I murmured, wondering again how I

could feel so welcome one minute, and like such an outsider the next.

"*Maman est stricte mais gentille,*" Marie-Claire explained with a little smile, glancing from me to the mother she'd just described as strict, but kind.

I nodded, but finished my pancakes in silence, still kind of afraid to say or do anything else that might make them dislike me.

My own mother liked to keep close tabs on where I was, and who I was with, but she and my stepdad had always been pretty casual about things like mealtime. Besides, with a baby in the house, it seemed that someone was always having to get up to find a washcloth, or heat up a bottle.

And while it wasn't exactly unreasonable that everyone remain seated until the meal was over, it did seem kind of impractical. I wasn't really a morning person. If I was going to have to allot an extra half hour to breakfast every day – instead of my usual five minutes for cereal – on top of waiting for the bathroom, I was going to have to start getting up pretty early.

I spent the morning unpacking and talking to

Mireille, who admired my clothes and held them up to see if they'd fit her. Apparently, she and Marie-Claire shared things all the time. I should have been flattered, but I bristled at the implication that she and I might also have to share. I'd already given her my mood ring, and donated my favorite turquoise, rhinestone-encrusted dragonfly hair clip to her little sister. Sharing – for a former only child – just didn't come as naturally to me as it did to the characters in the storybooks I read to Angelique at home. Sébastien, at least, had been happy with a quick drawing I made that featured him as a cartoon ninja fighter.

Sylvie, I discovered, worked from home on the computer. Mireille explained, as she rolled her eyes, that her mother was always available for the children, but also better able to keep tabs on them.

This, too, was new for me. My own mother had always gone out to work, and I'd had babysitters after school when I was little. Then, as I got older, I just came home by myself. A lot of adults seemed to think that was a bad thing, and that I must be very lonely, but I actually cherished my time alone, and did some of my best artwork during that time.

Which was why having Mom home all the time after my little sister was born actually turned out to be a huge adjustment. I wasn't used to having anyone home with me in the afternoons, and now that she was, she wanted a lot more say in where I'd been, what I ate, and how I spent my time. Yet it seemed that here, with my host family, things might be even more tightly controlled. I totally understood why Mireille had rolled her eyes as she talked about her mother "keeping tabs."

Just after lunch, we all piled into the van so that Sylvie could drop Mireille and me off at the high school, where we would meet up with the other exchange students and their partners. Mireille and the little ones continued to talk excitedly, but Sylvie – to me – seemed much quieter than she had the night before. I was sure this was because of the belly ring, and that she was wishing someone more wholesome, like Ashley, had come in my place.

Thankfully, as I arrived at the high school, Conner and I spotted each other at the same time. He smiled and greeted me not in French, but with a wordless hug. He held me for what seemed like a very long time.

Then, when he whispered into my ear, "You okay?" I

suddenly thought I might cry from relief. Mireille was wonderful. And I hadn't even been in Quebec for twenty-four hours. But seeing my friend, and hearing my own language again, was as comforting as hot cocoa on a cold day. With Conner, I didn't need to worry about first impressions, past mistakes, or being misjudged.

I swallowed, and whispered back, "It's hard." He nodded in agreement.

Reluctantly, I let go of him as Mireille approached, and fumbled through an introduction. When she looked quizzically from me to him, I thought I might have said things incorrectly again, but then she held out her hand toward him. "*Enchantée*, Conner," she said, her accent clipping the "C" on his name just as it did with mine.

She held his hand for much longer than I would have expected, and giggled when he identified himself, also, as "*enchanté.*"

"*Il a une blonde?*" she asked, under her breath.

"*Non*," I shook my head. He didn't have a girlfriend. "*Pas maintenant.*" Not right now, anyway, I said, remembering the girls he'd gone out with over the years.

"*Mais pas pour longtemps!*" she laughed, leaving me

wondering whether she might be right: Conner wouldn't be single for much longer.

* * *

The first afternoon had been designed as an opportunity for the exchange students and their hosts to get to know each other. First, our partners gave us a tour of the school. The building was quite new and modern compared to ours, something I found surprising for such a small town. I instinctively stuck close to Conner, but every time I looked up, anxious to make sure I hadn't lost him, he was already there. Having him near steadied my nerves.

Later, we played name games the way we used to back in grade school. Even though we were there to learn French, our teacher, Madame Poisson, told the French-speaking students to do their introductions in English, so it would all be more *juste*.

Everyone had to say their name, and then – in the language we were trying to learn – share something we liked (or loved?) that also began with the same letter as our name. One of the few things I found unsettling about the French language was the slippery meaning of the verb "*aimer*," which sometimes suggested love, but, more often than not, was simply about liking something. To me, they were very different concepts. But in the French language, it didn't seem like such a big deal.

Christophe began by telling us in halting English that he liked cookies. I knew I would remember that because his accent made it sound like "gookies," and I relaxed at the realization that Quebecois kids mispronounced words just as we did. His partner, Josh, liked *giraffes*, which made everyone laugh, because he was so tall, and we all knew it was probably the only thing he could think of in French that came anywhere close to the "J" sound he needed.

"*Je m'appelle* Caitlyn," I said when it was my turn. Then, relying on years of reading the bilingual text on my art supplies, added: "*et j'aime les crayons de couleurs.*"

"I am called Mireille," I heard my new "sister" say after me. "I like music, movies, and men." She smiled proudly, and then looked directly at Conner. Then I heard Conner say, "*Moi,* Conner, *aime* Caitlyn, *beaucoup, beaucoup.*"

Chapter 5

Hearing Conner tell all of the exchange participants that he liked me (*a lot, a lot*) was more confusing than anything anyone had said to me since my arrival.

"You said 'no boyfriend,'" Mireille whispered in English. I couldn't remember the right word for "later," so I settled on *après* (after), and she took the hint. I tried to concentrate on the names of the other exchange participants as they spoke, but focusing was impossible with Mireille on my left, and Conner – who liked (or loved?) me *beaucoup* – on the other side of her.

Madame Poisson kept us busy for another hour with trust exercises, like following our partners around blindfolded and falling backward into their arms. I studied Conner when he wasn't looking to see if anything had changed, but his face didn't reveal anything new or different. He had the same smile, the same relaxed expression. And when his eyes met mine, there was nothing in them that I hadn't seen earlier.

By the end of class, I had convinced myself that there hadn't been anything more significant than the letter "C" in Conner's choice of "Caitlyn" as the thing he liked *"beaucoup, beaucoup."* I said good-bye to him as always, noticing the warmth in his hand as he squeezed mine briefly on the way out. But then, for the first time ever, he brushed my cheek with his lips. It was a gesture I'd noticed many of the Quebecois guys made when they greeted or left their female classmates. But it wasn't anything I'd ever seen Conner do before.

On the way home, I did my best to join in the conversation, asking questions about the school and the town. Mireille mentioned nothing about Conner when her mother asked about the afternoon, but she did raise an eyebrow when I said nothing major had happened. Then, as soon as we were back in our room, Mireille almost pounced on me.

"Conner – *il est ton ami ou ton chum?"* she demanded, positioning herself in front of me on my bed.

"*Mon ami,*" I answered truthfully. He *was* my friend, and had been for a long time. He was not my boyfriend.

"*Mais il t'aime BEAUCOUP,*" she pushed. But even if I had known the words that could better explain our relationship, I wouldn't have shared them.

At home, I was the artsy girl who'd gone out with a guy I was pretty sure had cheated on me. A guy who'd humiliated me publicly, announcing to everyone at a party that I put out. A guy who'd hit me too many times before I found the strength to dump him.

I didn't want to be that girl anymore.

So I couldn't tell Mireille about the deep and sometimes complicated relationship I had with Conner. It was too hard to express, even in English, how Conner had stood by me during and after my nightmare with Tyler. How he had always encouraged me to be a better person. And, most importantly, the way he'd known, even before I did, that Tyler was dangerous.

"He's a good friend," I said.

She raised her eyebrows and shook her head. Mireille then proceeded to list the reasons that I should look beyond his friendship: "*Intelligent, gentil, beau.*"

I knew she was right. But he was still only a friend.

Then again, Tyler had been jealous of Conner when they'd first met, and I'd spent a lot of time trying to convince him that guys and girls really could be just friends. Now, I wasn't so sure. The part of me that was still angry and bitter about Tyler made me want to completely ignore Conner's declaration of affection rather than act on it, because that would only prove my ex-boyfriend right.

"*Only a friend*," I said again, probably trying to convince myself as much as her.

Shaking her head again, she took off the mood ring, and handed it back to me. "*Amour*," she said. At her insistence, I put the ring back on my finger, and watched it turn from blue-green to a dark purplish-blue.

"*Voilà!*" she declared, pointing to the ring color chart, which indicated that I was experiencing love, happiness, and passion. Her confidence reminded me of Ashley, and made me wish I could call *her* about it.

Love and happiness sounded great. But I wasn't sure I was ready for passion again. And what, exactly, would Conner be expecting? Like pretty much everyone else at school, he knew I'd gone all the way with Tyler. I didn't want him to think that I would automatically do the same with him.

Thinking along these lines triggered a slow blush that crept from the base of my neck up to my forehead the way watercolors spread across a wet page. Thankfully, Mireille couldn't have known why, and she interpreted it as me just being unconvinced.

"*Alors, on doit demander les étoiles ...*" she said decisively, leaping off the bed. In the time it took for me to look at my ring again, she was back with a teen magazine in her hand. Flipping it open to the second to last page, she scanned the horoscopes.

"*Ici!*" she said, pointing to my horoscope for the month of October, which was just beginning. I had trouble with some of the vocabulary, but the words "*spéciale,*" "*amour,*" and "*extraordinaire*" made it pretty clear that, if you were one to believe in astrology, this was going to be a pretty hot month for anyone born under my sign.

For the next hour, Mireille and I chatted as best we could about my love life. But we were limited both by my French and my uncertainty. She was sure that Conner had meant he liked me in a romantic way, but I was less convinced. And when I tried to consider the possibility that she might be right, I started feeling terrified.

"*Mais pourquoi?*" Mireille pressed, wanting to know why I was so scared. And I couldn't tell her, because I wasn't sure myself. It wasn't that I thought Conner would turn into a jerk the way Tyler had. And it wasn't that I was completely uninterested. It was more about *me* than about him. About whether or not I'd be able to give enough of myself to anyone ever again after everything that had happened.

Conner always said there were no mistakes in art. But there *are* mistakes in life. And sometimes, they hurt beyond belief.

Shortly before dinner, my mom called. "I just wanted to make sure you're settling in okay," she said. "And that you're getting along with Mireille."

"She's great," I said. She asked a few more questions, and I tried to reassure her that everything was fine. But her voice sounded tight and strange.

"Are *you* okay?" I questioned. "And Ashley's mom? Did you hear anything about her chemo?" I asked, suddenly worried that my mother's odd tone might have something to do with my best friend at home.

"Everyone's fine," she said, but she hesitated before she found her voice again. "Listen, honey, I'm sorry to be messing up your immersion experience by using all this English with you on your first day there. You got some mail this afternoon and I wanted to talk to you about it." She paused again, and I could picture her frowning, the way she did when she was thinking really hard about something. "But you sound so much more grown-up now that you're away from home ... I think I'll just take Mike's advice and forward it to you there. Okay?"

"Sure, but what is it?" I asked, thinking it was probably too early to have heard back from the most recent art contest I'd entered.

"Something good, I think," she said.

Chapter 6

*D*inner at Mireille's house that evening was even more chaotic than breakfast, so my mom's strange phone call was forgotten almost immediately.

Finally, I got to meet Mireille's other brother, Nicolas, who had been asleep when I'd arrived, and already at school by the time I woke up. He was thirteen, and, according to Madeleine, *pénible*. *"Pénible"* was a word I had never encountered, and when I asked Madeleine what it meant, she did a great monster impression, stomping around making growling noises. So at dinner, I was almost surprised to find that far from being awful and beastly, he was just as polite and giggly as the rest of the kids in the family.

The first thing he asked about was my age. Before I could answer, Mireille reminded him that he was not old enough to date under their parents' rules. And since I was his *nouvelle* sister, he shouldn't even be thinking about it. Hearing this, he grimaced and started gagging, which probably should have insulted me, but instead cracked me up.

"*Elle dessine très bien, c'est tout!*" he finally said, motioning toward the cartoon I'd drawn for Sébastien earlier in the day. "*Pour une ado.*" I was used to people being impressed by my artistic abilities, but it was still always nice to get a compliment, and it made me like him instantly.

I offered to draw something for him, too, after dinner.

"*Et moi?*" Madeleine asked. Her mother reminded her that I'd already given her the beautiful hairclip she was wearing, and she pouted a bit before pulling it from her hair and handing it back to me. "*S'il te plaît?*" I nodded, thinking about how hard it had been that morning to give away my ring and hair clip, but how both had come back to me.

After dinner, Mireille explained, we were going to be on dish duty. The little kids set the table, Marie-Claire helped out with the cooking a couple of nights a week, and Mireille and Nicolas shared the job of dishwashing.

That night, because it was my first evening with them, and because Nicolas and Madeleine were so anxious to have their pictures done, Marie-Claire offered to do the dishes for us.

I looked questioningly at the dishwasher, tucked in quietly under the cupboards, trying to come up with the right words to ask why they didn't use it, but Sylvie shook her head. *"C'est mieux quand on travaille ensemble."*

I didn't really see how working together could be better than using the dishwasher, but I didn't want to seem like I was criticizing them – especially since Marie-Claire was letting me off the hook for the first night.

Marie-Claire's generosity didn't end with her offer to do the dishes. After I'd finished making sketches for her siblings, she invited Mireille and me up to her room to go through her closet.

"You need to look very beautiful tomorrow," she said, holding up first one outfit, then another. "For Conner." I glanced quickly at Mireille, who smiled at me. Obviously, the two sisters told each other everything.

Finally, she picked up a fitted top that was a soft mix of turquoise and green, and held it up against my torso.

I liked the shirt. I knew the color would be beautiful with my red hair and light skin. But as I reached out to take it from her, I remembered a time when Tyler had thought something I was wearing was too low-cut. The top had been fine, but he'd always been jealous, worried that other guys – like Conner – were looking at me. He'd insisted that I change my clothes before we went out.

Nobody would have called the top Marie-Claire had offered overly provocative. But thinking about what to wear – what Conner would like – suddenly made me feel insecure in a way I hadn't been for months. And I didn't want to feel that way.

"*Merci*," I said, trying to find the words to say that I should save her generous offer for a special occasion.

"But the ring says you love him," Mireille pointed out, before speaking quickly to her sister in words I couldn't catch at all.

Marie-Claire was interested in the ring, too, and wanted to know where I'd gotten it. Uncertain of the words for fortune-teller or palm-reader, I used the words for "read" and "hand" along with "future." Not only did they seem to understand, they seemed to be more open-minded about fortune-tellers than Ashley had been.

"I think Conner is your love," Mireille said that night before we went to bed.

The next morning, I started classes at the high school. French was the only subject I would be taking with my fellow exchange students. First period was gym, during which we played soccer. Next, I had a free period before lunch. Mireille showed up and announced that Conner and his partner, Alexandre, had saved us seats in the cafeteria.

Part of me wished we could just talk normally, the way we always did. But another part was relieved to have to speak French, which meant we wouldn't be getting into anything deep. Like the future. Or love.

I stared at the lunch that Sylvie had packed for me, but I couldn't eat it. *"Il y a un problème?"* Mireille asked, looking questioningly at the ham and cheese sandwich I'd abandoned.

I shifted my eyes quickly toward Conner, who was laughing at something that one of the Quebecois girls had said.

Mireille grew quiet, and studied the other girl's body language. *"Elle veut ton chum,"* Mireille whispered to me when the girl had left. *Veut.* Wants.

I wasn't sure about the nuances of "wants" in French. Did it mean she wanted Conner *romantically?* I reminded Mireille again that Conner wasn't my *"chum."* But Mireille cut me off, explaining in further detail that the other girl – Roxanne – wanted to ask Conner out. *"Alors,"* Mireille finished, crossing her arms in front of her chest. *"Décide!"*

My ring turned the color of amber – unsettled – as I twisted it around on my finger.

"Décide," she mouthed again, standing up with her empty cafeteria tray.

But I wasn't ready to decide. At least, not right then and there. Not out of jealousy. Not while I was feeling homesick for everything familiar. Not without thinking through every possible plus or minus. And most certainly, not right before Conner and I began an afternoon of classes together.

Alexandre and Mireille walked Conner and me from our lockers down to our art class. We arrived just as Roxanne passed by and lifted her hand in a flirtatious wave. I kept my eyes on Conner, looking for a reaction. He smiled broadly, and waved back.

But he would have done so with anyone. It didn't *prove* anything. And, anyway, he'd said he liked *me*. Even if I wasn't sure I wanted him to.

Part of me was relieved when we discovered that we couldn't sit together in class. He took a table up front, and I sat closer to the sinks. The art teacher welcomed us, handed out paper, and had us spend the next eighty minutes sketching our shoes while classical music played in the background. I glanced around the studio, assessing the artistic skills of my new classmates and marvelling at how much their shoes communicated about their personalities.

The girl on my right had hippie-style sandals, worn over thick wool socks with a long, cotton skirt. Comfortable. A guy at another table wore black clothes over his heavy black boots. Angry. Conner wore basketball shoes, embellished with neon laces, safety pins, and doodles. Fearless. My own ballet flats felt like frauds. They wanted to dance, but instead, they hung back, not quite slippers, not really shoes. Undecided.

Conner waited for me when class was over, placing his hand on the small of my back to guide me through the crowded halls to our next class. It was a gesture he'd made before, but now it felt like a question.

Mireille was waiting at my locker after school, wearing a sly grin. "*Comment ça va?*" she asked teasingly, checking my ring. Then, before I could tell her I was fine, she told me she had planned "*une surprise*" that was going to be "*très amusante.*" I followed Mireille through town – wondering where she was taking me – on the bicycle that Marie-Claire had offered me for the duration of my visit. I thought about Conner and the Quebecois girls who were eyeing him. If Conner was really interested in me, he wouldn't be tempted to date the other girls. But if we really were meant to be, shouldn't I be more certain about what I wanted? As I pedaled, the voice in my head fell into a rhythmic *he loves me/he loves me not* refrain. And then, miraculously, as Mireille slowed her bike to a stop at the town's small harbour, I saw that Conner was already there waiting for us. *He loves me*, I thought, stopping beside her.

"*Salut!*" Mireille called out toward the other students who had gathered there.

At first, I didn't know what everyone was doing, but then one of the Quebecois guys whipped past me on his bike. When he got to the end of the pier, though, he didn't stop. He just kept riding until his bicycle flew off the edge, and both he and the bike landed in the water with a loud splash.

A cheer rose amongst the crowd. And while the boy in the water retrieved his bicycle and pushed it ashore, another one positioned himself to repeat the trick. Soon, everyone was splashing into the water one after another.

Mireille had joined the group as soon as we arrived, while I hung back, observing and calculating the risk. It was a warm day for the end of September. But still, the river had to be cold. The water where they were going in was probably ten feet deep. Too deep to stand up in, but not really safe enough for diving, it seemed to me.

The girls who'd already gone in stood laughing and shivering, their T-shirts clinging to their bodies. I didn't think I could be that uninhibited.

Mireille paused to brush the wet hair out of Alexandre's eyes just before throwing herself in the water too. Conner was already soaked, presumably from an earlier plunge of his own. I headed toward him, but then stopped when I saw that he was busy helping Roxanne pull her bike out of the water.

"Caitlyn!" Mireille called and pointed, indicating that I should take a turn. And when I hesitated, she began to chant my name, encouraging others to join her. "Cait-lyn! Cait-lyn!"

Peer pressure has a reputation for making people do things they later regret. *Tyler* had made me do things I regretted. To Tyler, I had been a possession. He told me what to wear, where to go, and who to talk to. And when I tried to express an opinion that differed from his, he often told me what to think.

I no more wanted to ride into the water because a crowd said so than I wanted to start dating Conner just because Mireille had told me to "decide." When I turned, I saw that Conner was chanting louder than anyone else for me to participate. I hopped on the bike and rode away.

Chapter 7

My dramatic exit was limited by the fact that I had nowhere to escape to. I didn't know my way around town yet, but I remembered how to get back to Mireille's house, so that was all I could do. I was hoping to sneak in quietly, so that I wouldn't have to explain myself to anyone, but Sylvie and the younger kids were already home.

"*Tu es toute seule? Pourquoi?*" Sylvie asked, wanting to know why I was all alone.

I didn't want to tell her about my overblown hissy-fit, and I didn't want her to think I had a problem with Mireille. I settled on a half-truth, and told her I was tired. She nodded knowingly, and didn't ask any further questions as I made my way to the room I was sharing with Mireille.

It wasn't long before Mireille returned home, wanting

her own explanation. *"C'est quoi le problème?"* she asked, peeling off her wet clothes and wrapping herself in a blue robe that matched her eyes.

Not sure how to say "I didn't feel like it," I shrugged.

"C'est amusant – fun!" she said, sitting down beside me. Then, taking my hands in hers, she waved them around, as if cheering for the activity I'd bailed on.

I knew she was trying to make me smile, but I couldn't. She sighed and crossed her arms in front of her chest. *"Conner l'a adoré ..."* she continued, as if she thought that because Conner liked flying into the cold water, I should too.

I shrugged again, and watched as my roommate shook her head in exasperation. *"J'aime m'amuser,"* she said. But I already knew that she liked to have fun. *"Et je veux m'amuser avec ma nouvelle soeur,"* she continued, making me feel guilty for not being the kind of "sister" she could have fun with.

"Désolée," I apologized, then tried again to explain myself by telling her how tired I was. But when she nodded, and apologized herself for making me uncomfortable, I felt worse. I started wondering whether she

would have liked Ashley better. And I wouldn't blame Conner if he decided he liked Roxanne better too.

* * *

At least Mireille didn't hold any grudges. *"Ton horoscope dit que tu vas avoir une conversation très importante,"* she teased me the next morning, showing me the newspaper. I wasn't exactly sure how much of an important conversation I would be able to have in French, but as it turned out, the stars were right.

Conner took me aside as soon as I arrived at school, whispering in English.

"What's wrong? Why did you take off like that yesterday?"

"I was tired ..." I said, trying out the same excuse that had worked on Sylvie. Conner, however, shook his head to indicate that he knew better, and expected more of an answer. My ring turned gray as I remembered the way he'd shouted for me to join in.

"I was afraid, okay?" I looked down at my feet. "And then everyone started yelling at me ..."

"You could have just said you didn't want to," he said, as if it would have been the simplest thing in the world.

"You weren't so supportive yesterday when you were cheering along with the crowd," I replied.

"Because it was such an adrenaline rush, and you would have loved it," he laughed. Then, he got serious again, and I could see that he really cared about my feelings. "But you could have just said 'no,' and just hung out with us. I didn't expect you to disappear completely."

"I guess I wasn't quite ready to face my fears," I said, remembering the way he'd taken Roxanne's hand as he pulled her from the water, but letting him think that I meant biking off the pier.

But even as I said it, his light touch and easy manner were making me think that maybe, with him, I didn't need to be afraid anymore.

* * *

That afternoon, in French class, Madame Poisson explained that much of her class would involve field trips and tours. She believed that the most effective way to learn a language and develop a sense of culture was to experience it, so she had planned outings to the local radio station, the bakery, and a number of other nearby businesses and landmarks.

"*Et notre première destination*," she said, pointing to the Saint Lawrence River on a map at the front of the room, "*est le fleuve Saint Laurent*." Because the river was so close to the Atlantic Ocean, she explained, it was salty and moved with the tides.

She gave us all a few minutes to grab our jackets from our lockers, and then we made our way down to the Saint Lawrence River. We were near the pier where everyone else had played the evening before. Everything looked different in the early afternoon, and I struggled to remember why the idea of joining in on the fun had felt so intimidating earlier.

I knew how much Ashley, a devoted animal lover, would have wanted to see the endangered beluga whales that were occasionally spotted in the water. Once again, as our teacher spoke of them, I felt guilty that Ashley wasn't able to experience this.

Then, my thoughts turned to the moonlit beach

where Tyler had taken me for my fifteenth birthday. He'd given me a goldfish as a present. "Goldie the Second" was – as his name suggested – my second goldfish. My first goldfish had been a gift from my real father when I was four, on the last day I ever saw him. Tyler had known this, and tried to replace something I'd lost. I couldn't have predicted, at the time, how much Tyler would ultimately take from me in return, but I felt it, there at the river, as I looked at Conner and wondered whether I would ever again be ready to fall in love.

I tried to follow Madame Poisson's account of how the river had opened the entire continent to its first European settlers, but the seagulls and the lapping of the tidewaters drowned her out. Try as I might to focus, I could think only of what it would be like to be with Conner, and yet how much I would lose if his friendship slipped away.

As Madame Poisson finished her lecture, I sat down on a rock, watching the water. Conner moved away with the rest of the group, down the sandy riverbank. Most of the others seemed to be looking for bits of shell and beach glass – fragments of broken glass worn smooth by years of tumbling around in the water. I'd gathered beach glass before, on Florida vacations with my mom. Greens and browns – from wine and beer bottles – were common. Sometimes I'd find clear bits, dark blue, or aquamarine. But most rare and special to me were the very few clear pink ones.

Sometimes, my mom and I would make a game of hunting for it. She'd offer to let me stay up late for bed if I could find three green ones in a row, or buy me an ice cream if I found a sapphire-colored piece.

Now, beside the river, I played the game again. Standing up, I told myself that if the first piece I found was brown, green, or clear, Conner and I weren't meant to be. If I found blue or aquamarine, I would have to think about it some more. But if I could find a pink one, the rarest of the pieces, I would take it as a sign that we were destined for one another.

Several times as I sifted through the sand and tiny stones, I thought I saw green flecks, but they all turned out to be nothing more than leaves or seaweed. Then, as I turned over a bit of brown shell, Conner reappeared, bearing a tiny piece of clear pink beach glass in his hand. It was no bigger than my thumbnail, but it was thick, and – if you used your imagination – almost shaped like a heart.

"*Pour toi*," he said, tucking it into my palm.

It was perfectly smooth. And in my hand, it didn't feel fragile at all.

Chapter 8

Before we left the river that afternoon, Madame Poisson announced that there would be a dance for the exchange students on Saturday. The theme, she explained, was "French Around the World." We were all encouraged to dress up like someone from a French-speaking country.

"You should go as a belly dancer from Tunisia," Mireille said, swaying her hips around when I didn't understand the French word for "belly dancer." "Then you could show off your sexy belly ring." "*Sexy*" – the English word – was a word the French-speaking kids seemed to use a lot. Obviously Mireille understood that her mother was not a fan of my piercing, but she always seemed to be trying to get me to show it off.

I clamped my lips shut and shook my head no. "*Et toi?*" I asked her, wondering what she was going to be.

Mireille looked up at the ceiling and thought for a while. "Maybe a girl in a bikini in Saint Martin?" I threw a pillow at her, and we laughed until we couldn't breathe.

In the few days I'd been living with her, I'd quickly discovered that although Mireille's parents were somewhat traditional, their strict approach to parenting seemed to make their children all the more eager to push the limits. Although neither of the older girls was involved with anyone, Marie-Claire and Mireille seemed totally guy-crazy. They were also in great shape, and had no worries whatsoever about flirting and flaunting their bodies – as long as their parents weren't around. And I had no doubt that if she could have kept it a secret from her parents, Mireille would have happily attended the dance in an itsy-bitsy bikini with a belly ring of her own.

I wondered whether that was always the case with girls and their mothers. Ashley, for example, had a very liberal mother, who had been married three times, and had offered to buy birth control for Ashley the minute she'd started dating. Yet Ashley had wanted to wait until she felt ready and the time felt right. Consequently, she and Brandon had never gone all the way.

And my own situation was probably the craziest. Because my mother had been young and unmarried when she'd become pregnant with me, she'd always encouraged me to wait, citing many of the obstacles she'd faced as a single mother. But she'd also been a realist, telling me from an early age that I could talk to her about sex and birth control when the time came, because she wanted me to be able to make informed decisions.

And yet, I hadn't talked to her about any decision, informed or otherwise, because when the time came, I didn't get to decide anything. I was forced.

Later, my therapist assured me that it hadn't been my fault.

And I understood that it wasn't. But it struck me as ironic, in a way, that even by not choosing my own path, I was just like Ashley and Mireille, doing the opposite of what my mother had wanted most for me.

Mireille nudged me, and my thoughts returned to the present.

Together, Mireille and I brainstormed possible costumes. Then, I had an idea. *"Une personne qui passe les cartes dans un casino de Monte Carlo!"* I said. Going as a couple of blackjack dealers from the aristocratic French casino, Monte Carlo, would be perfect. Mireille's eyes flew open wide, and she bit her lower lip. "*Non!*" she said. "*Maman dirai 'non.'*"

"*Pourquoi?*" I asked. Sylvie was strict, but Mireille couldn't have known for sure that she would automatically say "*non.*"

Mireille didn't explain, but continued to shake her head 'no.'

In the end, Mireille told her parents that she'd been "assigned" to wear a costume that represented Mardi Gras in New Orleans. She went clad in a slinky, beaded dress of Marie-Claire's with a feathered mask she borrowed from a friend. Despite her pleas for me to try something *plus sexy*, like a Swiss ski bunny or a princess from Monaco, I ultimately settled on being the chicest of the French – fashion designer Coco Chanel.

"I thought artists were creative," Mireille complained when I told her I was going with a simple black and white dress I'd found at the thrift store. It would have looked better on Ashley's model-perfect figure, but it was classic enough for anyone to pull off.

"Fashion designers are artists," I said. "We study them in art class. And Chanel was the twentieth century's most talented designer."

"But it's boring ..." she said, looking puzzled.

"Elegance through simplicity," I repeated the Chanel quote I'd learned from my favorite art teacher, Mrs. Van der Straeten.

But in truth, it wasn't as simple as I pretended.

I'd actually put a lot of thought into how I wanted to project myself, and what I should wear to do that. Mireille wanted to look "available" – which she was. I wanted to look "mature" – which I was trying to be. We were the same age. But sometimes, because of my experiences, I felt years older.

Marie-Claire helped with our makeup, and Madeleine trailed behind us as we prepared for the dance, spinning around and demanding to know why she, too, couldn't attend *"la fête."* With three teenage girls now in the house and only one bathroom on the upper floor, I'd quickly adjusted to the "open door" policy when it came to personal grooming such as brushing teeth and applying makeup. It was the only way everyone could get in and out on time. It was also when we socialized, talking about the day ahead, or what we'd dreamed about the night before, as we scrubbed our faces and combed out our wet hair.

"*Attends!*" Madeleine called out when we were ready to leave. She wanted to see what color my ring was. To everyone's dismay, it was gray.

Little Madeleine looked confused, wanting to know if it meant that I didn't love Conner anymore.

Mireille explained that it just meant I was nervous. Then, unfastening a chain from around her neck, she asked for my ring, and motioned for me to hold my hand out flat, palm facing upwards.

"Should Caitlyn be with Conner?" she asked the ring, and it slowly began to move. A year ago, I'd done the exact same thing in front of my mom's pregnant belly. If the ring on the chain moved in a circle, it supposedly meant "yes" to whatever question had been asked. A straight line meant "no." Over and over again I'd asked variations of "Is it a girl?" or, because my mother was carrying a test-tube baby and I was a little freaked out, "Is it a human?" Each time, the response from the ring had matched up perfectly with what the ultrasound had already – scientifically – confirmed.

I watched nervously as the ring began to vibrate first a little, then more, until it was circling around in an undeniable loop. All the way to the dance, I thought about the way my ring had swung around to indicate "yes," Conner and I should be together. I'd been thinking about him ever since he'd given me the perfect piece of beach glass. The ring's prediction gave me courage. It also steadied my nerves when Conner showed up shirtless in a grass skirt, face paint, and a feathered headdress.

Always a nonconformist, he'd come as a Haitian witch doctor. Instantly, I found myself falling under his spell.

"*Enchanté*, Coco," he said, acknowledging our shared art background through his instant recognition of my costume.

"You are so different," Mireille murmured, looking again at my stylish dress and looking back at Conner. "But right for each other."

At first, the DJ played fast music, so there wasn't much opportunity to talk. Then, as the first slow song began, Conner reached for my hand and pulled me toward the dance floor. I couldn't believe how perfectly I seemed to fit with him, wrapped up in his arms.

There was definitely something different about his eyes – and it had nothing to do with his face paint. It was the way he was looking at me, as if he wanted to say something, but didn't know how. And now, after hesitating for so long, I wanted to help him.

Closing my eyes, I relaxed, and allowed myself to stop thinking for the first time all week. Then, when the music ended, I took his hand, and led him out into the hallway.

He smiled slowly, realizing that I was holding his hand in a different way, and used his other hand to touch my face. A shock ran down my spine and I suddenly realized that yes, there were lots of things I wanted to do with Conner that "friends" didn't do.

But that meant I would never be able to call him "my friend" ever again.

"I can't do this in French," I whispered.

"Do what?" he asked.

"Ask you what's happening with us," I said, forcing myself to meet his eyes again. "And tell you that I'm terrified."

He pulled away for a moment, with a look of concern

on his face. "I don't want you to be terrified."

"Maybe terrified isn't the right word," I admitted, looking down. "Just scared. Of messing up our friend-ship ..."

"I know," he said, nodding.

"And ... of getting hurt."

He studied his hands for a minute. "I will *always* be your friend, Caitlyn. No matter what. And if you're not ready for a different kind of relationship, I totally get that. I don't want you to do anything you aren't comfortable with."

And as he said it, I heard the genuine concern in his voice. My fear of missing the chance to be with him started to outweigh my fear of messing things up.

"I need to switch back to French for a minute," I said, taking a deep breath.

"Why?"

"To do this."

Then, I leaned in, and kissed him. His tongue was warm on mine and tasted sweet. When we finally pulled apart, I said the only thing I could think of.

"Caitlyn *aime* Conner. *Beaucoup. Beaucoup.*"

* * *

I went home to Mireille's that night feeling like everything was unfolding just as Madame Syeira and my horoscope had predicted.

"I told you!" Mireille squealed from her side of the room after I'd spilled all the details of what happened. She spoke so quickly that I could hardly follow her words, but I knew she was happy for me, and it doubled my happiness to have someone to talk to about it. I wanted to talk to Ashley, too, but it was late, and I still wanted to savor the evening a bit.

All night long, I replayed the soft, slow kiss in my mind. Tyler had been the first guy I'd really kissed. There had been times when I'd felt certain that I would never do anything so wonderful in my whole life as making out with him. But kissing Conner was different. Tyler – I recognized now – had kissed hungrily, greedily, working his tongue in my mouth as if probing for something he couldn't find. Conner kissed with confidence. His lips were soft on mine, and his touch was gentle.

I hadn't realized, until it was too late, that Tyler had

been a jerk. And, now that I knew the difference, I also realized that he had been a terrible kisser.

I couldn't wait to see more of Conner, but fate dictated otherwise.

On Sunday, I was expected to go to church with my host family. The sermon itself was long, and difficult to follow because so much of the religious language used odd words and verb forms I hadn't yet learned. By the time we'd attended service, and the coffee hour that followed, the entire morning was gone. Then, we spent the afternoon outside, raking the leaves that covered the grounds around the house.

I didn't honestly expect to enjoy any of it. But in the church, I was able to study the way the light filtered in through the stained glass windows, spilling colors onto the parishioners below. And I knew that my friend Conner – my *boyfriend* Conner – was the only one in the world who would understand how much beauty I saw there.

When we were done raking, we all went inside for hot chocolate and pumpkin carving. I was covered in leaves and aching from the work, and though I still wished that I could have spent the day with Conner, I didn't mind waiting either.

Once, when Tyler and I were together, Conner had told me that love should make me feel good. At the time, I hadn't understood that because I thought I *was* in love and that I was happy. Now, I knew differently. With Tyler, everything had always seemed urgent and dramatic. I felt as if I had to talk to him or see him all the time. I couldn't yet say that I was *in love* with Conner, but I didn't need constant texts and e-mails to prove that we liked each other. I just knew we did.

I decided against saying anything to Ashley about the fortune-teller's prophecies when I finally e-mailed her on Monday afternoon, keeping things factual, even understated. Still, when she responded a few days later, she made a few predictions of her own:

I know you regret a lot of things that happened with Tyler, but remember that your mom found a really good guy after your dad left. I think that's proof that you can learn from your mistakes and make better choices (even if my own mom is still looking for Mr. Right). Conner's ideal for you. It might sound dumb, but I've always thought that the way he puts other people first with little things, like holding the door open or saying "thank you," kind of shows that he is considerate by nature. That counts for A LOT in a relationship. Plus, he's kind to animals :). So as long as you're CERTAIN that his electric blue hair comes out of a bottle, and not a bad gene pool (in case you want to have kids with him some day in the distant, distant future ...), you should go for it. Thanks for sharing this amazing news with me, even at the risk of getting caught by the English Police!!! I wish I could be there with you.

The bit about animals made me laugh. Conner *was* going to be good for me. Meanwhile, I had come to care very much about Mireille and her family. But still, I missed my best friend.

I had just finished one full, perfect week in Quebec, and it looked like things were going to stay that way. But then, I received the mail my mom had told me about when I had first arrived.

Chapter 9

The letter was tucked inside a large yellow envelope. At first glance, I assumed that the mail Mom had forwarded was nothing more than a belated birthday card from my aunt. Until I saw the sticky note she had attached to it.

Hi Sweetie,

I hope you find good things in here.

Love, Mom

And then, I saw the name on the return address.

Scott Collins. My biological father.

My hands trembled as I carried the envelope back to my room, wondering what was inside, but afraid to find out. I had neither seen nor heard from my birth father since I was four years old – and I'd hardly even known him then. But now, out of the blue, he was writing to me.

But maybe not entirely out of the blue. I turned the

envelope over in my hands, examining the tight, tiny letters printed in pen. And for a moment, I wondered whether my mom might have had something to do with my father's sudden reappearance. She *had* blamed herself for my problems with Tyler, and many times she'd said stupid things like "If only your father had been involved in your life, you might not have gotten involved with such a control freak." As if a dad I didn't know actually had anything to do with my idiot boyfriend.

Mom had always said she didn't know where he was or how to get in touch with him. But they did go to the same college, and this was the digital age. She regularly complained that her alumni association was always phoning for donations and offering to reconnect her with old classmates. She might have contacted him through them. But what would she have told him? Would she have told him about every stupid move I'd made the year before, from skipping school to ending up feverish from an infected belly ring? And then, there was the question of my "relationship" with Tyler. That last night we'd been together, when he'd bragged about me "putting out" (against my will), and hit me at a party, everyone had found out about Tyler's abuse. It was bad enough for everyone at school to know, but for that to be my dad's reintroduction to me would be humiliating.

My mouth was completely dry as I opened the letter, and I was so overwhelmed that I had to read it three times before I really understood what it said. But by then my concerns were entirely different.

> *Dear Caitlyn,*
>
> *Today is your sixteenth birthday, and I find myself – as I often do – wondering how you are. It's hard for me to imagine you all grown up because you were so young the last time I saw you. I know that you must be very beautiful by now, because you were an adorable baby, and a gorgeous little girl.*

Right away, I felt myself bristle at the way he was focusing on what I must look like, as if that was the most important thing about me. I continued reading.

> *I don't even know if you remember me, and that's entirely my fault. I'd like to fix that now, if*

you'll let me. I've reached a place in my life where I would really like to know you better, or at least apologize in person for not being there for you while you were growing up.

Right, I thought bitterly. And *I've* reached a place in my life where I've finally learned to love my stepfather. And to accept the fact that you totally abandoned me.

I've included my e-mail address here in case you'd care to reach me. But I will certainly understand if you don't.
Love, Dad

After twelve years without contact, I wondered whether he even understood the meaning of love.

There is a moment before you begin a painting when the canvas is fresh and unmarked, the brushes are clean, and you know in your mind's eye *exactly* how you want it to turn out. And when everything goes perfectly, when you capture what you've envisioned, there is no better feeling.

But sometimes, after you start, your brush slips, or the

colors you mixed aren't right, or the perspective becomes distorted. Then, you have to decide whether you can work with what you've got and find a way to see it through, or whether it's always going to feel like a disappointment because it didn't turn out the way you had anticipated.

For me, that letter was like facing a pristine canvas. Except I had almost no control over the outcome.

I didn't have grand expectations of my father. I knew I'd been an accident, and I knew he ran out on us. I *had* wondered about him over the years. But if I responded to his letter, and he turned out to be even worse than I imagined, the last tiny possibility of a positive outcome would vanish forever.

The answers to all the questions my mother never wanted to discuss were just an e-mail away. If I booted Nicolas off the computer, I could satisfy a lifetime of curiosity in a matter of moments.

But my chest tightened and my throat burned as I thought about responding to the letter. I suddenly felt like a statue, unable to move, think, or even respond when Mireille came in. She immediately knew something wasn't right.

"What is wrong?" she asked in English, trying to make me feel more comfortable.

"My dad – my biological father – wrote me a letter," I explained in a shaky voice.

"It is good news, *non*?" she smiled broadly, then frowned. "So what is the problem?"

Once again, I wasn't sure whether I was having trouble communicating because of language, or my inability to identify precisely what was bothering me. Mireille was wonderful. But she had a perfect family with two parents who loved her, and brothers and sisters galore. I just wasn't sure that she could relate. "No problem," I told her. "I just need to call my mom."

* * *

"Oh, honey, I've been waiting for you to call," my mother said soothingly when she heard my voice. "What did he say?"

"Just wished me happy birthday. Said he'd like to get to know me. He sent his e-mail address." I picked at a flower printed on the bedspread while I waited for her reaction.

"Well, I'm not going to say 'it's about time,'" Mom said with just a touch of bitterness in her voice. "But I am glad to hear that *maybe* he's finally grown up. Did he say anything else? Like what he's been doing all these years?"

Her words and expression made it obvious that she hadn't, as I'd suspected, been in contact with him. The letter had been just as much of a surprise to her as it had been to me.

And maybe I should have realized it sooner, but I had grown up a lot during the past year, and it suddenly occurred to me that to my mom, he wasn't *just* my father. He was her first love. She didn't ask specifically, but she must have been wondering whether he'd ever married or had more kids. Even though Mom and Mike had been married for a long time, and had had Angelique together, my biological father's reappearance was probably much weirder for my mom than she cared to admit. I mean, I *hated* Tyler, but I still found myself wondering about him sometimes, especially when I'd see a car like the kind he drove, or heard something on the radio that I knew would interest him. Those kinds of reminders must have been so much worse for my mother, raising me alone and not knowing where my father was.

"He didn't say anything about himself at all," I told her, still picking at the bedspread. "And he didn't really ask anything about me, either. He just said he remembered my birthday and wondered if he could get to know me. So I don't really know anything that I didn't know yesterday except for his e-mail address. And I have no idea what I would even say to him ..."

I heard my mom sigh, and I pictured the *"Oh, honey"* face that she often gave me. "I *am* glad he contacted you, Caitlyn. But don't feel that you have to respond to him if you don't want to. Take your time. He certainly took his. At the very least, you should sleep on it."

It was good advice. But I couldn't decide if waiting was the right thing to do. So I tossed a coin, and when it landed heads up, I followed Mom's advice.

Chapter 10

"You actually flipped a coin?" Conner asked the next day, grimacing. We only had a couple of minutes outside the school before we went in, and I wanted to use some English.

"Yes," I said, raising my chin a bit defensively. "I couldn't decide what to do."

"Why not?" Conner asked as he stared at me. His face, which had somehow become even more handsome since the night I'd first kissed it, was framed by a maple tree in blazing fall colors of yellow and orange.

"Because I don't know what he wants from me, because I don't know what he's like ..."

"But you can't know any of that unless you contact him," Conner said gently, cupping my face in his hands.

"But what if he hates me? Or I hate him?"

"What if you like him and he likes you?" he

countered, moving his hands onto my shoulders. "Sometimes you just have to take a chance."

I pressed my lips together. I'd taken chances. Lots of them. I'd given them too. Like the first time Tyler had hit me. I'd accepted his apology and his promises to change after he begged for forgiveness on my doorstep in the middle of the night. But ultimately, he'd done it again. I *had* taken chances, and I'd ended up hurt both physically *and* emotionally. Sometimes you do have to take chances. And sometimes you just have to protect yourself.

Conner pulled back and squinted at me. "You didn't flip a coin to decide whether or not you'd kiss me the other night, did you?"

"No," I said. It wasn't a lie. And although he might have considered my private beach glass game to be just as lame, he was the one who had brought me the piece I was looking for. That had to be fate.

"Good to know. But now that your dad's finally stepped up, what's to decide?" Conner asked.

"Just if I'm ready to contact him or not. But it's hard." I sighed. "I wish I could be less emotional and more analytical, like Ashley."

"Well," he asked, taking my hand and walking me into the building, "what would Ashley do?"

I laughed, thinking about the time she'd taken an online test to decide whether or not she was in love with Brandon. "She doesn't like to go into anything until she has all the facts. She'd Google him."

"Okay, why don't you try that?" he whispered so that we wouldn't be caught speaking English. "Then maybe when you know something about him, you'll feel more comfortable contacting him."

"I've already tried the Internet ... lots of times, over the years," I whispered back. "But his name's just too common. Last time I checked, there was a politician, an author, a couple of teachers, and a whole bunch of other random people who shared his name. I could never tell which one might be him ..." My voice trailed off as I remembered the envelope in which his letter had arrived. It had been postmarked "Tofino, British Columbia." If that was where he lived, the new information might have given me exactly what I needed to narrow down my search. If I also searched under his e-mail address, I might find out whether he blogged or used any social networking sites, like E-Me. Either approach might give me the background information I needed to make me feel okay about following up with the stranger who was my dad.

Conner looked at me expectantly. "We're going to the computer lab for free period, aren't we?"

It only took a couple of attempts to reference his name and location. My mouth went dry as I read the first article, from a newspaper archive almost a decade earlier.

Man Convicted of Hit-and-Run Released

Scott Collins, 25, of Tofino, B.C., was released on probation yesterday after serving just two months of a two-year sentence. Collins was convicted on charges of driving while impaired and failing to remain after his involvement in a school bus accident. Collins was attempting to pass a stopped school bus, when he hit Sara Neal, 8, who had just exited the bus. Neal spent several weeks in a coma before regaining consciousness. As conditions of probation, Collins agreed to participate in several hours of community service, and to undergo counseling for alcohol abuse. The Neal family could not be reached for comment.

At news so horrible about the man who was my father, I would have expected to feel shock, disillusionment, and disgust. But in fact, I felt almost nothing.

That's what I told myself anyway.

I'd had years and years of practice telling people I didn't have a dad – or, at least, not one that cared enough to be a part of my life. So, usually, I could just rhyme it off matter-of-factly, as if I was talking about the weather or a book I wanted to buy. And by just saying it, without thinking about it, I usually didn't get emotional about it.

So the only real disillusionment or anger I felt as I read the article related to myself. I'd let myself hope that my dad had matured, and now understood the concept of responsibility. Hoping was my mistake.

Otherwise, I felt numb. The sounds in the computer lab faded away and everything suddenly got blurry. A tiny voice in the back of my mind, alternating in French and English, took on the rhythm of my breath. Stupid. *Stupide.* Stupid. *Stupide.* Stupid. *Stupide.*

I don't know how long Conner stood behind me before I noticed his hands smoothing my hair, his lips close to my ear, whispering low. "At least now you know why you didn't hear from him."

"Well, then hopefully he's smart enough to know

why *he* won't be hearing from *me*," I said, trying to hold onto the numbness.

Conner sat down next to me and gave up all pretense of speaking in French. "What – you're not going to contact him now because of some mistake the guy made in his twenties? This article's ten years old. You can't hold something like that against him now."

"Of course I can. I don't need anyone in my life with issues like that. He abandoned the girl he ran over, just like he abandoned my mother and me," I said. "Does that have a statute of limitations too?"

Conner exhaled deeply and took my hand. "You wanted some information so you wouldn't be going into this completely unprepared. You have that now. You may not like it, but you could at least send him an e-mail. If you don't think he deserves a second chance, maybe ask him why he thinks he does."

And just like that, the numbness morphed into anger. I wanted to scream at the absurdity of Conner's statement. Why did the rules always slip and change depending on what other people wanted? *"How can you be friends with Ashley after she criticized our relationship?"* Tyler had demanded. *"How could you have given Tyler a second chance after the first time he hit you?"* my mother had asked me over and over again.

Because, despite what they tell you in children's books, nobody really believes in second chances. Except Conner, who was suggesting, for reasons I could not at all fathom, that I should give my absentee, deadbeat, jailbird father another chance.

Chapter 11

*A*s time went on, I became even more certain that not contacting my father was the right thing to do.

Sometimes, I'd start to wonder whether I should be more forgiving. But whenever I did start to question myself, I'd put my ring back on my necklace, and use it as a pendulum the way Mireille had done the night of the dance. No matter how I worded my questions – Should I contact my dad? Am I right to cut him out of my life the way he cut me out? – the pendulum always confirmed my own gut feelings. No contact.

The more I watched Gilbert with his wife and children, the more I believed that my own father – even if he hadn't been a criminal – could offer me little besides further disappointment. When Gilbert came home at night, the little ones ran to him, and either climbed onto his lap or wrestled with him on the couch, until everyone was squealing with delight. Nicolas sat with his dad almost every evening, working on math problems he said he didn't understand. But I suspected that he just liked spending the time with his father. Marie-Claire and Mireille were more grown-up in their interactions, asking his advice or playing cards with him, but they, too, shared a special relationship with their father. And Gilbert always made time to speak directly with me, asking me how my day had been, or whether I'd heard from home.

My own father had skipped out on all the fun things when I was little. He'd skipped the hard parts too – like when I was sick, or upset. And yes, he'd even managed to miss the whole horrible Tyler-era. His reappearance now reminded me of how the animals in *The Little Red Hen* had all wanted to eat the bread when it was ready, even though they hadn't helped with the farming or the baking.

I didn't owe him anything. And yet, I couldn't stop thinking about him.

* * *

I hadn't given Mireille all the details about *why* I'd decided not to contact my dad, but I had told her that I just didn't feel ready. At first, she seemed to understand, but she picked up the subject again one day after school.

"Your ring is very black," she commented after she found me listening to my MP3 player in a corner on the dining room floor. "All day, whenever I looked at it, it was black."

I'd noticed the same thing. I looked at it more closely. "Maybe it's broken," I said doubtfully.

"Or maybe it's not the right decision?" she asked, sliding down to sit beside me. "Because you don't seem to be very happy."

A couple of days earlier, I'd been proud of the way I was getting along in a "French only" environment. Now, I just felt irritated by my inability to say the things I wanted to say. I couldn't tell Mireille, but I needed some space. As fun and easygoing as Mireille was, I still wasn't used to sharing a bedroom with someone else. I longed for the kind of privacy I had at home, in my own basement bedroom, where I could turn on any music I wanted as loud as I wished without having to check with someone else. Where I could start a painting, and leave it on my easel to add to and change it whenever I walked by it. And where, if I wanted to think, I didn't have to slink off to a corner in a dining room where I would, inevitably, still be discovered. At home, I could just *be*.

None of that was possible as a guest in another girl's room.

And though I wished I could, I didn't feel comfortable inviting Conner over. Mireille's parents had been clear from the start that he was welcome to visit, but only in the public areas of the house. It was as if we were being constantly monitored, when these days, all I wanted was some more privacy.

"*C'est le même avec nous,*" Mireille apologized when I told her I wished Conner could come by. She explained that Marie-Claire had only been allowed to go out as part of a group until she was seventeen. Even before that, she had learned the hard way that sneaking around was nearly impossible in such a small town, where their parents knew everyone.

* * *

On Saturday morning, Mireille suggested taking the little kids to the library for a story-time program.

"If we take them, Dad goes with Nicolas to hockey and Mom pays Marie-Claire to help clean the house while we're out," she'd laughed. "And we can use the computers at the library. It's good for everyone."

The library was quiet. Although I didn't have solitude, at least I had a little peace.

Not having been on the computer all week, I found my inbox full of jokes and e-mails from my mom. Ashley had sent a couple of short messages telling me about *Camelot*. But when I logged onto my E-Me account, I was stunned to see a bunch of freshly posted pictures of her acting crazy at some beach party. Usually – as I'd recently pointed out to Conner – she was very controlled. But the photos, which had been posted by another girl at school, showed her laughing and being silly. I was relieved that she was having a good time at home, despite having to miss the exchange. But I was still surprised to see her looking that spontaneous. In some of the pictures, she was pretending to pose like a model. In others, she was cozying up to Taiton, a guy who was also in the musical with her. This gave me the perfect excuse to call her.

She answered after a couple of rings, and claimed I hadn't woken her up, but I could hear her yawning and knew she was lying. That was also very unlike her. It turned out the party had been the night before, and she didn't know anything about the pictures yet.

"Well," I said. "There's a picture of you in Taiton's lap, so you'd better dish."

"There's nothing really to tell," she said. "He flirts a lot, but we haven't moved out of the 'just friends' stage. To be honest, I don't really know what he's thinking."

I brushed off her questions about Conner, and told her about the card from my dad.

"Wow, that's amazing!" she said, to my surprise. Ashley could be pretty judgmental under certain circumstances, and even without knowing about his DUI, I had expected her to say it was *"too little, too late."*

All of the frustrations I'd been holding in converged in that instant, and I ended up taking things out on my best friend. My voice got shrill and irritated as I described the article I'd found, and my subsequent decision not to contact him.

"What if something happened to him, though, and then it was too late to change your mind?" she asked. "Like, what if he ... got cancer or something?"

That completely threw me off. Would I feel differently if he was sick or dying, like Ashley's mom? I wasn't sure, but I didn't think so. It wasn't like he'd ever done anything for me, so I owed him nothing. On the other hand, I asked her, "What if I'd had cancer during all those years I never heard from him?"

Ashley talked a bit more about second chances, and I resisted the urge to point out how stubborn she'd been when her own boyfriend of two years had wanted to "take a break" and "see other people," and she'd broken it off completely rather than hanging around for him.

But almost as soon as I'd hung up, I regretted the conversation. I'd gotten defensive, and I hadn't asked her anything about her mom's situation, even when she brought up cancer. I wasn't doing such a good job at being a friend.

Thinking I might do better if I could write to her, I logged back onto E-Me, and sent her a message.

Thanks for listening this morning. Sorry I didn't really get a chance to ask you about your mom or tell

you more about Conner or Mireille, but I have been using way too much English lately. Anyway, except for the thing with my dad, things are mostly good here and I was glad to hear that they are going well for you too. Hope your mom is okay. Sorry if I seemed grumpy.

Love, Caitlyn

Then, I tried to be funny by commenting on a couple of her pictures. In one, she was pretending to model, and she had one hand on Taiton's chest, with her tongue sticking out as if she was going to lick him like an ice cream cone. It was obviously intended to be a joke, because Ashley had done some real modeling for a major agency over the summer, so I wrote: **I can't believe you used to charge people for what you're doing here for free!**

All the way back from the library, I was still thinking about Ashley and the funny way the universe seemed to work. It was almost as if nobody was ever allowed to be too happy, and if they started to be, something happened to shake them up. Like my drunken jailbird father trying to work his way back into my life just as I'd finally moved on from my worst year ever.

But sometimes, fate seemed to work out in the

opposite way too. Like when Ashley's mother got cancer, and her boyfriend dumped her. Just when things seemed to be the most discouraging for her, she'd been discovered as a model. And even though she hadn't been able to go on this exchange, which was awful for her, she ended up with the lead role in the school's musical. Judging by the pictures online, she was having a great time too.

As we walked home, with Madeleine and Sébastien chattering excitedly about the library, and with the last of the falling leaves whipping past us, Conner and Alexandre phoned and suggested a double date for dinner and a movie.

I felt perfectly happy.

And being perfectly happy made me perfectly certain that something bad was about to happen.

Chapter 12

I didn't have to wait long for that uneasy feeling to be confirmed.

Just before the guys arrived to pick us up, I logged back onto E-Me to check my horoscope and daily lucky numbers. But once again, I was distracted from doing so by the shock of Ashley's photos. After me, dozens of other people had commented on them, so that my entire notification page was filled.

To my horror, I saw that almost everyone back at home had completely misunderstood my comments about Ashley's pictures. Somehow, they'd gotten the impression that the things I'd said about Ashley getting paid to model versus "doing it for free" referred to sexual favors. Another comment I'd made – **Could you spread it around any more?** – referred to a photo where she had popcorn all over her hair and on the ground around her. Like the other comment, it had been similarly misinterpreted – or deliberately twisted – to make it seem like I was referring to her engaging in slutty behavior.

It was possible that like me, some of the first people to comment were trying to be funny. But as the comments kept coming, they grew increasingly crude and nasty. It made me feel sick inside to see what I'd inadvertently started.

The worst part, for Ashley, would be that the things people were saying about her were so far from the truth. Even after two years together with Brandon, I knew that they had never gone all the way, or even done a fraction of the other things people were referring to. And yet, the stuff on E-Me made it seem as if she'd been with every guy at school.

And although I deleted my own comments, there was nothing I could do about the others. I didn't even know what to say to her, but I knew I didn't want it to be public. When she didn't answer her phone, I switched over to e-mail to send her a quick apology.

"I'm the worst friend ever," I whispered to Conner on the way to dinner.

"I'm sure she knows you didn't do this deliberately," he tried to reassure me. *But I should have known better,* I told myself over and over. *I should have thought about what I was writing before I wrote it. I should have thought about who might see it, and how they might interpret it.* And then, maybe because I was already feeling low – or maybe because it was always there, just under the surface – I found myself thinking about my biological father again. It should have been obvious, when he dropped out of my life, that I wouldn't exactly feel like just calling him up years later because suddenly he wanted to reestablish contact.

Living in such a small town without a car meant our dining options were limited. There were several diners that served breakfast and lunch, but most of them closed down in the evenings. The pizza place was strictly takeout, which had left the four of us with only one choice: *Chinois*.

The restaurant itself was dated, but clean. Brown paneling ran around the walls, and the brown Formica tables had colorful laminated placemats explaining the Chinese zodiac in English. We studied it for a bit, with Conner and I doing our best to translate for Alexandre and Mireille for a change. Because the Chinese zodiac was based on year of birth, rather than month, we should, in theory, all have had the same personalities. But there were a lot of characteristics assigned to each animal – including a "can be" section that seemed to indicate opposite characteristics. So in the end, even though we all had very different personalities, each of us was able to find at least a couple of things in the description that applied to us.

"That's how these things work," Conner said. "They make it all so vague that anything they write applies to anyone who wants to believe in it." His skepticism surprised me, and reminded me of Ashley.

"Well, maybe with this one," Mireille agreed. "But the regular zodiac is much more accurate."

I thought she was right. For instance, after discovering the mess I'd made for Ashley, I realized that my online horoscope had said it was an important day to "think before you speak." I wished I'd read that earlier, but now, I heeded its advice and sat there quietly. At the end of dinner, though, my fortune cookie insisted that "my heart will always make itself known through words." So I tried to get in touch with Ashley again, but my calls still went straight to voicemail.

Like the restaurant, the town's only movie theater – which played only one movie per week, on Friday and Saturday nights – had seen better days. Two elderly women sold us tickets and popcorn, while an old man showed us into the theater. Mireille explained that the man was married to one of the women, who was the sister of the other woman, and the three of them had been running the theater together for fifty years.

The movie itself was really hard to follow because French was dubbed over the English-speaking actors, so their lips didn't match the sounds coming out. And yet, it was still one of the best movies I'd ever been to. Mireille and Alexandre flirted, while Conner and I held hands, whispered a bit in English, and kissed from time to time. Still, I couldn't stop thinking about the horrible E-Me comments I'd unwittingly unleashed. By the time we got back to our house, Alexandre and Mireille were "sort of" going out.

Once Mireille's parents learned that we both had new boyfriends, they decided to invite them to dinner later in the week.

Worried that Madeleine might say something over

dinner that we didn't want the guys to know, Mireille and I prepped her in advance to avoid certain topics completely.

The conversation was comfortable until we began talking about my baby sister, and the fact that my parents had let me name her. Madeleine pouted, and said *she* wanted a baby that *she* could name.

Everyone laughed, and Sylvie shook her head.

Not one to give up, Madeleine looked alternately at her two big sisters. *"Marie-Claire? Mireille? Pouvez-vous m'obtenir un bébé comme celle de Caitlyn?"*

The older girls laughed again – their little sister wanted them to have babies just to indulge her.

"Jamais avant le mariage!" Sylvie exclaimed, shaking her head. Marie-Claire rolled her eyes, as if to say "we know, never before marriage." But Sylvie's face looked serious, full of warning.

I almost choked on my food, and actually coughed a bit more than necessary, hoping to change the subject. My mother hadn't been much older than Marie-Claire when she'd had me. Unwed.

"Mais, pourquoi?" Madeleine wanted to know why.

"C'est une erreur," Sylvie said brusquely.

Clearly, it wasn't perfect that my parents hadn't been married. And yes, my birth father had been a selfish jerk who'd taken off because of the unplanned pregnancy, and failed to keep in touch for twelve of the sixteen years I'd been alive. But still. My own mother had always been very careful to never describe me as a "mistake."

Conner must have been thinking the same thing. "*Caitlyn n'est pas une erreur. Elle est fantastique!*"

I appreciated Conner trying to come to my defense. But I couldn't sit there, with everyone looking at me. So I broke the cardinal rule that everyone had to stay seated during dinner and mumbled "*Excusez-moi*" as I left the table.

Chapter 13

*O*nce again, I found myself upset, and unable to go anywhere that I could be alone. I grabbed my jacket, and headed for the backyard swing set.

Several minutes later, Conner appeared out of the darkness and sat down on the swing beside me.

"They didn't know," I told him. "I mean, Mireille did, but I never discussed my birth father with Sylvie or Gilbert or any of the other kids."

"Oh," he was quiet. "I'm sorry. I didn't realize. My host parents know pretty much everything there is to know about me. I assumed you'd gotten close to Mireille's parents too."

"We kind of got off on the wrong foot," I explained, thinking about the belly ring fiasco. "And besides – I'll probably never see them again after I leave here anyway."

Conner frowned. "That doesn't mean you shouldn't give them a chance to get to know you. You can't just assume that they won't want anything to do with you after you go home."

His words hung in the air for a moment while I tried to wrap my head around what he might really be saying.

"Still," I tried to change the subject. "It wasn't your story to share."

"No, it wasn't," he acknowledged, taking my hand. "It was never a secret before, so I didn't realize you wanted to keep it private. I'm sorry."

My fingers felt stiff next to his, but I didn't pull my hand away. Instead, I let him keep talking.

"And besides – it's nothing to be ashamed of."

"I wasn't ashamed," I said quietly. "Not before, anyway. But Sylvie and Gilbert are so perfect ... and they have this great family."

"You have a great family, too, remember?"

"Kind of. But it's ... it's like a rainbow without the purple streak on the bottom layer. And I never really noticed that before. But now that I realize it's missing, I can't stop noticing that it's incomplete."

He rubbed his thumb against mine, and I felt my body relax.

"So why won't you invite the purple back?" he asked.

It was a question I'd asked myself *mille fois* – a thousand times – since receiving my father's letter.

"Because purple's the darkest shade in the rainbow," I admitted. "And it's got a lot of blue in it. I don't think I can take any more blue in my life."

* * *

"*Je veux te parler* ..." Sylvie said to me, when I finally reentered the house. Because I was still hurting from her words, *I* didn't want to talk to *her*. And my first instinct was to pretend I didn't understand. But she'd said it so slowly, and so pointedly, that I couldn't fake my way out of it.

I followed her into the living room, which, for the first time I could remember, was quiet and empty. Apparently, the rest of the family had been instructed to leave us alone.

I kept my eyes on my hands, and traced the band of

my darkened mood ring as she spoke.

"*Je suis vraiment, vraiment, désolée,*" she began. She continued to speak in French, but slowly so that I could understand her. "I didn't mean to criticize you or your family."

I nodded, to indicate that I already knew she hadn't done it intentionally.

"So please, accept my apology. I didn't mean to be judgmental," she explained. "I only wanted to reinforce, for my girls, that all choices have consequences. Good or bad."

I tried to wipe a tear out of my eye without her noticing, but she saw, and reached behind her for a box of tissues, which she passed to me.

After a moment of silence while I got myself together, she continued. "Gilbert and I wanted you to be very good friends with Mireille. So we didn't push to spend time with you. But now maybe it's time for us to get to know each other better. Please – will you tell me more, yourself?"

Cautiously, I started by telling her about my little sister, and how worried I'd been that she would end up being the favourite child, because she had been planned.

But Sylvie shook her head, and said, "That would be impossible. A mother loves all of her children. Differently, sometimes, but still, she loves them all." She smiled, and put her hand on my cheek. "Even the daughter she gets to have for only a few months," she said, referring to me.

"I know that now," I told her while I squeezed her hand. "But at the time, I was worried because she was having Angelique with my stepfather, and my own dad was out of the picture."

Her expression became one of confusion, tempered with concern.

"He didn't have a lot to do with me, when I was little," I explained. "But I did see him, once in a while. And then, when I was four, he stopped all contact, and just kind of – disappeared."

"How terrible for you!" she said, squeezing my hand.

I nodded. "It was confusing. But I got used to it." Sylvie smiled sadly, as if to say she wanted to be supportive, but didn't really believe that anyone could "get used" to their dad not being around.

"You never heard from him again?" she asked, shaking her head.

I exhaled sharply, and told her more. "Not until my mom sent that letter. It had a card in it, from my dad. For my sixteenth birthday."

Sylvie smiled broadly then – a genuine smile, that included her eyes. "How wonderful!"

I shook my head. I wasn't yet ready to admit the news I'd discovered about him, but I could be honest about my feelings. "I think it's too late. I don't think he deserves another chance."

She didn't try to change my mind, but nodded, to indicate that she understood what I meant.

"*Et ta maman?*" she asked. "*Qu'est-ce qu'elle dit?*" I explained that my mother had told me to take my time deciding if I should respond.

"Mothers always want what's best for their children," she said, echoing her earlier words.

And that, I thought, was the difference between a parent like Sylvie and my own absent father.

Chapter 14

Since we'd already had a costume party at the beginning of the exchange, Madame Poisson planned something entirely different for Halloween. Each of us was assigned a location in town that was said to be haunted. It was up to us to interview one or more of the townspeople about the history of our "haunt," and write a brief description about it.

"Ta recherche est un secret!" Madame Poisson cautioned. We couldn't tell anyone else what – if anything – we discovered. Then, on Halloween night, we would work in groups of four to complete a ghostly scavenger hunt. The object of the game was to be the first team to answer assigned questions about each haunted location. And the only way to answer them correctly was to visit each spot, where the question would be posted along

with a summary of the story.

"*Je n'aime pas les fantômes!*" Madeleine had declared when we explained why we couldn't take her and Sébastien trick-or-treating. I laughed, wanting to reassure her that ghosts weren't real, even though I felt an ominous chill in the air that night.

My spooky location was a small wooded area just at the edge of town. One night after dinner, I sat down with Sylvie and Gilbert to find out what they knew about the story.

Decades earlier, on a winter's afternoon, a woman and her husband went hiking through a wooded property, looking for a place to build their matrimonial home. When she needed a bathroom break, she headed off the path for some privacy, telling him to continue ahead. A long time passed, but she didn't return. Eventually, her husband went looking for her, but the falling snow had covered her tracks. Nobody ever saw her again.

Kind of like my dad, I thought bitterly.

Heartbroken and still desperate to find her, the woman's husband purchased the property, and searched every day for some trace of his lost love. In time, though, he married again. And on his wedding night, he looked out the window and saw an eerie green light winding its way through the woods.

He tried to follow it, but every time he came close, it vanished.

The light haunted him for the rest of his life. Every time something joyous happened in his life, like the birth of a new baby, or a successful business venture, the light would reappear, tainting the good event with memories of the life he might have had.

"*Y croyez-vous?*" I asked, wondering whether Sylvie and Gilbert believed it.

Sylvie smiled. "*Je pense qu'il était hanté par le regret.*" She thought he was haunted by regret, and her words reminded me of Ashley's advice when I had called to tell her about my father's letter. Then, as if she could read my thoughts, Sylvie took my hand. "*C'est possible que ton papa soit hanté par le regret aussi. Tu peux lui donner de la paix.*"

Maybe she was right and my father did have regrets. But it wasn't up to me to give him peace. And besides – *I* was the one fighting off ghosts.

* * *

On Halloween night, everyone gathered in the school parking lot. Madame Poisson gave out maps and a sheet with the questions, and wished us luck on our quest to find *un fantôme*.

The last of the daylight was fading over the town. As the first evening stars appeared, I focused on one – avoiding the area of the sky where *my* star, named by Tyler, would be. Then, I began to make a wish, as I'd often done when I was Madeleine's age:

Star light, star bright.

First star I see tonight.

I wish I may, I wish I might

Have the wish I wish tonight.

But I chickened out, as always. I didn't wish for anything specific, such as "true love," "wealth," or even "happiness." Instead, I wished that I knew what to wish for.

Ashley never would have made such a wish, because she was independent, and didn't want to have things decided for her. I did because I could never decide on anything.

Conner, Alexandre, Mireille, and I, bundled up warmly in heavy coats, set out on foot to find the assigned locations. As usual, we all spoke in French, but by now, it almost felt natural.

I was surprised by how many murders, accidents, and other untimely deaths there had been in such a small town, but Alexandre reminded me that it was an old settlement, so there was lots of history.

"Everyone's got secrets, right?" Mireille said, and I leaned into Conner, hoping she wouldn't realize how right she was.

The last stop on our ghost tour turned out to be Madame Poisson's house, in which, according to legend, a child had died of whooping cough years ago. The last owners of the house had claimed they heard a death rattle almost every night, but it stopped when they discarded an iron bed frame stored in the attic.

We joined our classmates in Madame's kitchen for hot chocolate and cookies. Then, Alexandre suggested we stop by his house on the way home.

"Will your parents allow it?" I whispered to Mireille

as we grabbed our coats.

"I already called *Maman* to say that we are with Madame," she said, grinning.

Alexandre's parents were far more relaxed than Mireille's. They had no problem whatsoever with the four of us heading downstairs, unchaperoned, to the basement. In the spirit of Halloween, Alexandre turned down most of the lights, and dug out an old Ouija board.

"You go first, Caitlyn," Mireille said when we were trying to think of a question to ask the spirits.

"I don't know what to ask ..." I confessed. *And, not asking is easier than getting an answer you don't want to hear.*

"Okay, I'll go," Mireille said. I expected her to come up with something flirty, like, "Does Alexandre love me?" but she surprised me by asking "Do ghosts exist?"

As per Ouija board tradition, all of us had to rest one hand on the pointer, and wait for the spirits to guide it toward "yes" or "no." At first, nothing happened. Then, slowly, the pointer began to turn and slide toward "yes." Everyone accused everyone else of moving the pointer themselves. But when I felt a shiver run down my spine, I wasn't so sure.

After a couple of more questions, the guys went upstairs for drinks and snacks. Then, Mireille asked the Ouija board about me and Conner.

"*Est-ce que Caitlyn et Conner sont destinés l'un pour l'autre?*"

The pointer glided effortlessly under our fingers, and I felt again that it was moving on its own.

"I told you," she said smugly. "Conner is your soul mate."

I hadn't questioned it since the night he'd been over for dinner, but it was reassuring to think the spirit world might be rooting for us.

"Okay – so if you guys still don't believe in ghosts, do you at least believe in reincarnation?" Mireille asked when the guys had returned.

"Not really," said Alexandre.

"Me either," Conner added.

"I don't know ..." I admitted, considering the possibility. "But wouldn't it be great to know we could all get a second chance at happiness, in case our first life doesn't work out very well?"

"I disagree completely," Conner said. "Because if your life isn't going well, you have to be accountable for it, and look for ways to improve it. You can't just wait around wishing for things to be different."

Or wishing you knew what to wish for, I thought to myself, remembering the first evening star.

But the fact that my boyfriend and I could express our true opinions to each other meant that in a lot of ways, things were different.

* * *

In late November, the school arranged a four-day field trip to Quebec City for all of the exchange students and their partners. It meant we had to spend another few hours on the bus. But this ride was very different from the one that had brought us to the town. Now, Conner and I were a couple.

Alexandre had saved seats for the four of us across the back of the bus, as far away as possible from the driver and chaperones. Conner had brought a small blanket along, so we could snuggle together. The ride passed quickly.

On the way into the city, we stopped at a famous cathedral called *Sainte-Anne-de-Beaupré*. The entrance was filled with crutches, which Madame Poisson explained had been left by people who had supposedly been cured of illness and disease just by visiting.

Inside, the lights were dim, and we had been cautioned to be respectful of the visiting public, who were there to pray, not to tour. Conner put his arm around me as we entered, and hooked his thumb into my pocket.

The sheer size of the cathedral and its soaring, vaulted ceilings, was awe-inspiring. I felt immediately drawn to one of several small tables covered by flickering candles in colored glass votives. Each flame, the bilingual write-up explained, represented someone's prayer on its way up to heaven. Ashley was the first person to come to mind as I stood there contemplating what (if anything) I might pray for. Silently, I dropped some coins into the collection box and lit a candle for Ashley, asking that whatever harm I might have done to her not cause lasting damage. Then, I lit another for her mother, asking for her chemotherapy to be successful. And as I contemplated what it would mean to my best friend if she were to lose her mother, I thought about what it had meant for me to grow up without a father. I saw myself as the little girl I was, crying when the goldfish my father had given me floated belly up to the top of the bowl. I hadn't realized until that moment, there in the cathedral, that it wasn't the fish I'd been crying for.

And I didn't know if praying for yourself was allowed, but I took a chance that it might be, and lit my last candle, asking for healing from the scars that I hadn't known I carried.

Conner never asked me what I'd been praying for. I didn't say it, but he seemed to know what I needed. He led me through the sanctuary, showing me carvings and intricate tile mosaics, and paintings with eyes that seemed to look right at us, no matter where we stood.

The most amazing thing about the whole place, though, was the whispering posts. Architecturally, they were columns supporting arches in the ceiling. But just like the play telephones we'd made as kids out of string and Styrofoam cups, the pillars carried sound vibrations between them, transmitting the slightest of whispers from one listener to another, several feet away.

The posts, Madame Poisson explained, had been designed back when communicable diseases, like smallpox, were a big concern. Rather than putting priests at risk of infection from the sick in a confessional, people whispered into the pillar, which transmitted their voices clearly, but privately, to the priests listening from a safe distance.

Conner and I hung back, waiting while the others in our group tested them. Then, when the last of them had moved on, we positioned ourselves to try it.

"What are your confessions?" I asked teasingly with my lips right next to the pillar, before pressing my ear against it.

"I confess to lustful thoughts," he whispered back playfully. "And thinking about you all the time, even when I'm supposed to be doing something else."

"I confess to the same sins," I whispered back, then found myself tearing up at his reply.

"They're not sins, Caitlyn. If anything, they're blessings."

Chapter 15

$\mathcal{A}$fter checking into the hotel, our group walked downtown for dinner at a fondue restaurant beneath Quebec City's castle-like hotel, *Le Château Frontenac*.

"It's about time I took you out on a proper dinner date with real tablecloths," Conner joked as we sat down in the elegant restaurant. Mireille announced that if your meat fell off of your fork into the fondue pot while it was cooking, you had to kiss someone at your table. Then, to make her point, she purposely dropped a piece of meat directly into the pot, and proceeded to kiss Alexandre on the neck.

"I don't need any excuse to kiss Caitlyn," Conner said, pressing his lips to mine while the chaperones weren't looking.

"Get a room!" someone from another table yelled

toward us and I wasn't sure whether they meant Conner and me, or Mireille and Alexandre. But for once, we *had* a room.

After dinner and a tour of the boardwalk next to the *Château*, we had free time at our hotel before lights out.

"I'm going up to see Alexandre," Mireille declared almost as soon as we'd returned to our room, while peering into the mirror and smoothing her hair. "So maybe you could keep Conner down here."

"How come?" I asked Mireille's reflection while applying lip gloss. Standing around together in the bathroom while we primped had become so normal, I could hardly believe it had seemed strange to me that first day at her house. Then again, my French skills had progressed to the point where I could speak without really having to think about it.

"Because I want to be alone with Alexandre," she said coyly. Her voice was so suggestive, I froze out of surprise. I hadn't realized that she and Alexandre were that serious. Mireille saw the look on my face, and blushed. "You want to be alone with Conner, too, don't you?"

I didn't know what I wanted. I'd wondered what it

would be like to be alone with Conner, testing the boundaries in my mind. I trusted him, and I might possibly even have loved him. But now that we would actually have to chance to be alone, I found myself feeling short of breath and jittery.

I was still thinking about the possibilities minutes later, when I opened the door to Conner's tentative knock and sheepish grin.

"Hi," he said, bending down to kiss me. His hands were warm on my lower back as he held me close and smiled. I studied the angles of his face, and wished I could paint him that way – happy and relaxed with his eyelids half closed, looking down at me. I knew now what people meant when they said that love brings out the best in you.

As I reached up to brush the hair out of his face and kiss him again, he looked down, and moved his hands across my stomach. "You're so beautiful," he whispered. I lowered my eyes, trying to see myself the way he did, and caught the faintest glimmer of my belly ring. An image of Tyler kissing it, shortly after I'd had the piercing done, darted through my memory. I pushed the thought away, and clung tightly to Conner.

It had taken years for us to move past friendship, into romance, and months for us to find ourselves alone. In a strictly linear sense, our relationship had moved at a snail's pace. I liked and trusted Conner. And I wasn't doing anything I hadn't done before. But as he wrapped his arms around me and we moved closer to the bed, it felt as if things were moving too quickly.

Suddenly, I was paralyzed with fear. My body tensed and I couldn't breathe, speak, or move.

Immediately sensing my discomfort, Conner pulled away. "What's wrong?" His eyes were wide at the sight of the tears that had started falling down my cheeks, as he brushed them away gently.

Despite hours of therapy, and repeated assurances that what had happened with Tyler *wasn't my fault*, I felt ashamed to admit the truth. And the truth was, once, I'd been helpless, pinned under a jerk who hadn't listened when I'd said "no."

In those first few seconds when Conner had pulled me close to him, I'd been taken back to that dark place and time.

"I – I can't do this. Now. With you." I managed to squeak.

"Do what?" He kept his eyes on mine, searching for clues.

We'd had a teacher one time in health class who'd told us that if we were too embarrassed to talk to our partners about what we were doing, then we probably weren't in a mature enough relationship to be doing it with them in the first place. At that moment, I knew she was right. I struggled for the words to tell him what I meant.

"You know," I said, dropping my voice to a whisper. "Go all the way. I'm sorry."

"Oh Caity," he said, pulling my face into his chest and kissing the top of my head. "I didn't expect you to! You're ... we're not ready." He pulled back, and looked me in the eye. "You thought that's what I was planning?"

"I kind of thought *I* might want to," I said, using my finger to trace the fleur-de-lys on the front of his souvenir T-shirt. "I thought you did too."

He chuckled. "Well, yeah – of course I *want* to. Someday. When we're both ready. Which we aren't." Then, he asked me if I'd ever heard of "The Marshmallow Test."

"No," I confessed, wondering what marshmallows could possibly have to do with us.

"Well, they did this study with little kids, in the 1960s," he explained. "And they told them that they could have a marshmallow. But the kids were also told that the researchers were leaving the room, and that if the kid could wait, and not eat the marshmallow before the researcher got back, they'd get two marshmallows, instead of one."

"And?"

"*And* seventy percent of the kids they tested couldn't wait. They only got one marshmallow because they didn't have the self-control to wait an extra fifteen minutes. But the ones who did wait got the two as promised."

I still wasn't following. "So?"

"So we may be in the minority," he said softly, "but good things come to those who wait."

"That's what my horoscope said last week," I told him. "But for today, it said 'This will be a good day to connect with others,'" I laughed. "Maybe I didn't have to take it so literally."

Conner perched on the edge of the bed, and motioned for me to sit beside him. He kissed my neck. "You don't really take any of it seriously, do you?"

"Umm – sometimes," I admitted. "Like the costume

party night, when I kissed you? I wasn't sure if I was ready to take the next step or not, but my horoscope said the stars were perfectly aligned for romance. Or something like that." I rubbed my fingertips along his forearm, but he pulled away.

"You told me you hadn't flipped a coin to decide about us, but that pretty much comes down to same thing, don't you think?"

I tried to read his tone, but it was hard to do, because his words were so unexpected and I couldn't see his face.

"How can you trust anybody when you don't really trust yourself?" he asked, sounding puzzled. When I didn't respond, he continued, softly. "What if your horoscope had said 'Be wary of romance?' or 'You will meet a tall, dark, handsome stranger?' Would I even be here right now, Caitlyn?"

I stood up to face him. "Of course you would."

He chewed on his lip for minute. "I'm not so sure about that. You still haven't contacted your father because he lost that coin toss ..."

"You *know* why I didn't contact him," I said bitterly, crossing the room.

He shook his head. "No, actually, I don't. You say it's because he's a drunk and a criminal, but you tossed that coin before you ever found that out. Your mind was already made up."

"It wasn't made up – that's why I did the coin toss!" I crossed my arms and practically shouted at him. Out of the corner of my eye, I noticed that my mood ring was darker than I'd ever seen it.

He saw me shift my eyes in the ring's direction, and a sound that wasn't quite a cry escaped his lips. "You're so scared of taking a chance on anything that you can't make a move until you get the okay from your horoscope. Or a coin toss. Or a fortune teller who probably couldn't read Ashley's future because she didn't have anything different to say than what she'd already told *you*," he said, standing up. "And that's really sad, Caitlyn, because you're a smart girl. But you need to decide for yourself whether or not you really want to be in this relationship. Nothing and nobody else can do that for you."

And just like that, he walked out of the room, leaving me alone to figure out what I really wanted.

Chapter 16

As soon as the door slammed shut, I burst into tears. Hours later, when Mireille reappeared just before curfew, I was still trying to figure out what had happened. I was well past feeling shy with her, but the whole thing felt impossible to translate.

"*Il était furieux?*" she parroted back to me with a confused look on her face.

I nodded. "But ... why?" she tried again, in English. She was trying to reach out to me, and I needed that, more than anything.

"Did he want ...?" she started to ask, putting her hand on my shoulder.

"No," I said. "But I thought I did. And then I didn't. And then we got into a fight about why I'm so indecisive about everything."

"Conner is kind," she said, tilting her head to one side. "Why are you so indecisive?"

I took a deep breath, and spoke honestly with my friend.

The two of us stayed up all night talking. She cried with me as I described the humiliations I endured as Tyler's "girlfriend," and how scared I'd been of an unplanned pregnancy or disease after he'd forced me into unprotected sex.

"I always wanted to let it just *happen*, when the time was right," Mireille admitted. "So it would be romantic. But Marie-Claire said I need to be ready in advance." She sighed. "Now I can't be so spontaneous. But I know to protect my body."

"You do need to protect your body," I agreed, sniffling. Then, remembering just how much harder it was to break up with Tyler once he'd had all of me, I asked, "But how will you protect your heart?"

"It will be harder with my heart," she admitted. Then, she shrugged. "But now I know that that is important too."

Ever since my arrival, I'd carefully guarded the

secrets of my past, fearing that Mireille would judge me for them. Now, I thought maybe it wasn't judgment from Mireille or anybody else that I had feared, but judgment from myself.

"*Merci,*" I said, hugging her. "*Pour tout.*"

All night it snowed, and by morning a thick layer of white clung to the window.

"So," Mireille said, as the sun tried to peek through the glass. She was still showing her support by speaking in English. After so many months spent struggling to understand what was going on around me, I loved her for it. "Now you will call him?"

"If he wants to talk to me, he'll be in touch ..." I started to say. But I was interrupted by a low rumble as a small avalanche of snow tumbled down the side of the building, clearing our window as it fell. And in that moment, I began to see clearly what Conner had meant about deciding things for myself. I didn't need to wait for him to call me. I needed to take control and call him first.

I dialed expectantly, but when he didn't answer his cell phone, I sent a text. When he didn't respond to that, I called his room.

Alexandre answered sleepily. *"Âllo?"*

"Désolée," I apologized. *"Conner? S'il te plaît?"*

I heard some mumbling, then Alexandre's scratchy morning voice saying: "He says he doesn't want to talk to you right now," he said.

So much for "always being friends" no matter what happened romantically, I thought, feeling hurt.

Our class was scheduled to spend the day involved in activities requiring small groups, so the exchange participants and their partners had been split into two teams. My group, which was spending the day at the Quebec Circus School, had to leave earlier than Conner's, which was having a guided tour of the old part of the city. The next day, we would switch.

The Quebec Circus School was exactly as its name implied, a school for teens who someday wished to (literally) join the circus. People who attended classes there enrolled in an academic program that also included arts and athletics. It was primarily focused on such arts as clowning, dance, and acrobatics. None of which I was in the mood for.

All through the performance of acrobatics, I thought

about what had gone wrong with Conner, and whether there was anything I could say or do to make it right. I knew exactly what Conner had been upset about, but still, I continued looking for answers in chance occurrences unfolding around me. *If that guy does a jump while he's on the tightrope*, I told myself, *then this is just a little blip in a great relationship. But if he goes straight across, or starts walking backwards, Conner doesn't want anything else to do with me.*

I hated that I was doing it, but watching for "signs" had become almost as natural as breathing. And when I didn't see the ones I wanted – which happened often – I changed my own rules, deciding, for example, that the tightrope walker didn't have to jump on the first crossing, and the second or third would still count.

After the show, we went into a practice area, where we could safely experiment with a lot of the apparatus ourselves.

Mireille must have seen the horror on my face as I watched our classmates clamoring to spin in a sling-like trampoline. She squeezed my hand and hauled me over to the stilts.

"*Essaye*," she commanded, and I wondered whether or not it was coincidence that the French word for "try" was so close to "easy" in English. It was certainly ironic. Just because I tried something didn't mean that it would be easy. My love life was proof of that.

Still bargaining with myself (but also not willing to try the tightrope, despite its close proximity to the padded floor), I decided – illogically – that if I could learn to walk on the stilts, it would be a sign that Conner and I could at least still be friends.

I started by leaning against the wall, but collapsed onto the mats before taking a single step. Again and again, I tried, but I couldn't help but fall.

And although I wanted to believe that "practice makes perfect," I already knew from the aftermath of my disastrous love life that that was entirely untrue. So I wasn't surprised either when despite my best efforts, I failed to master the stilts, or when my calls to Conner continued to go unanswered.

It was late in the afternoon when we returned to the hotel, and already growing dark. Conner was waiting outside my hotel room door when we arrived.

He stood and offered me a hug. Smiling, Mireille slipped quietly away, and, though I tried not to, I burst into tears.

"Hey – it's okay," Conner said. "What's wrong?"

My sadness morphed into disappointment as I looked into his handsome face and knew I couldn't kiss it anymore. "I'm sorry, okay?" I said. "I'm sorry I pissed you off and ruined our relationship, but you *promised* to always be my friend – you could have at least answered my phone calls ..."

He shook his head. "No – I couldn't. I dropped my phone in the fountain last night and wrecked the battery. Didn't Alexandre tell you that this morning?"

"He just said you didn't want to talk to me ..."

"I'm sorry," he said, touching my cheek with his finger. "Something must have been lost in translation. I was in the bathroom blow-drying the phone, and I said I didn't want to talk to you *right then*, because I was coming down to see you in person anyway. But then when I got to the lobby, your group had already left."

My bottom lip started to quiver with the hope that things might turn out to be okay.

"Of course I want to be your friend, Caitlyn," he said, putting his hands on my shoulders. "I still want to be your boyfriend too. I just want you to be sure that it's what *you* want, and not what some mood ring or pendulum says you should do."

I nodded, and threw my arms around him, crying again with relief. "It *is* what I want. I didn't mean to hurt you when I told you about the horoscope and stuff ..."

"I was hurt," he said, shaking his head, "but it never even occurred to me that our relationship was ruined. I meant what I said about learning to trust yourself. Not everyone's going to leave you, Caity," he smiled, and I thought about his words as he continued. "In fact, I want to take you somewhere before dinner. I want to show you something."

We bundled up in our winter coats and boots, and ventured out into the old part of the city. Conner led me past historic buildings dressed with white lights and cedar boughs. Some were already adorned with twinkly ice sculptures, though the winter *Carnaval* was still months away. In Place Royale, the oldest section of the town, the moon was just coming up over the stone church, and it was bright enough to cast our shadows on the snow.

Finally, we arrived at *Place de Paris*. We stopped in front of a sculpture depicting nothing more than a small white block on top of a larger one, crisscrossed with black lines that made a grid like you'd see on graph paper. After witnessing so much historical beauty in the city, its newness was a shock.

"It's called *Dialogue with History*," Conner explained. "And when France gave it to Quebec City in 1987, people were expecting something grand and ornate, like the Statue of Liberty that France had given to New York. When the unveiling took place, though, somebody turned to one of the dignitaries from France and said, 'I can't wait to see what's in the box,' not realizing that the box *was* the sculpture."

I nodded, recognizing that it wasn't the kind of eye-pleasing art most people would appreciate. Then, I circled around it, looking at it from every angle. "But no matter what an artist wants to convey to the viewer, people will always take from a work of art only that which is meaningful to them," I said.

"Exactly," he agreed, taking my hand in his.

"And maybe, fortunes and horoscopes are the same way," I said slowly, thinking out loud.

"I was using them to confirm what I already wanted. I was so afraid to take a risk that I just told myself that we were destined to be together."

"Maybe," he said, wrapping me up in his arms. "But anything that brought you to me has to be at least a little bit magical." He kissed the top of my head as the snow began to fall again.

I examined the sculpture further, looking for the meaning I could take from it. It was the epitome of simplicity. Once, like most of the world, I'd believed that anything simple was of little value. I'd believed artists had to struggle to create masterpieces, and people had to work hard at building strong relationships. But since I'd been with Conner, I'd learned that the good things, like great art and unbreakable bonds, could also come easily. Being with Tyler had been complicated. Being with Conner was simple. And that made it good.

The sculpture before me, by sheer virtue of its simplicity, was also elegant, gutsy, thought-provoking, and utterly unique. People might forget which sculpture depicted Samuel de Champlain or Jacques Cartier or any of the city's other celebrated founders. But nobody who saw it would ever forget *Dialogue with History*.

And what was it our history teachers were always telling us? That, like the little block the sculptor had placed on the larger one, our futures are always built upon the past. So if we don't learn from history, we are destined to repeat it.

"How can we both see all that in two little cubes, and *not* be destined to be together?" Conner asked, as we walked back toward the hotel.

"We can't," I said. "And you can't say stuff like that and then tell me that you don't believe in destiny," I teased.

Later, as we passed the fountain in the lobby, I asked him how he'd managed to drop his phone in it.

He grinned sheepishly. "It fell out of my pocket when I tossed in a coin, to make a wish." I laughed, but he continued, squeezing my hand. "And it turns out that tossing a whole phone in might actually be luckier than just using a penny."

Chapter 17

*A*nother letter awaited me when I returned to Mireille's home from Quebec City. This time it was from Ashley. Although there hadn't been any E-Me-related problems since the pictures had been pulled down, she'd been vague in the few conversations and messages we'd shared since. I was eager to read what she had to say.

Dear Caitlyn,

I know e-mail is quicker, but I also still think there's something magical about receiving actual mail (not bills or junk), and since you are about to come home, I figured that if I was ever going to write to you, I should do it now. (Besides, I am at the hospital, without a laptop, watching over my mom while she sleeps, so I actually have time to do this!)

I'm sorry that I've been kind of out of touch lately. As I said above, my mom has been in the hospital. She had pneumonia, as a side effect of the chemo, but it's clearing up now. I have also (obviously) been crazy busy with rehearsals for the musical. We ended up with a last-minute cast change, and the drama wasn't all onstage – but I'll tell you more about that when you get home.

I can hardly believe that you will be home in three weeks! I hope that you have had an amazing time, and I can't wait to hear all of the details.

Also, since I haven't heard anything else about it, I assume that you didn't end up contacting your dad. But I wanted to apologize if you felt that I was trying to pressure you that day when I was talking about the possibility of cancer and genetics and stuff as being good reasons to meet him. I was just really frustrated with my mom's situation, because I've been thinking a lot about how I could lose her to this awful disease. If I was in your place, I would want to meet my other parent while we were both still healthy, if only to get any important family health history. But when I said all that, I was thinking about myself, not you. I can't begin to know what it has been like to grow up without having him around, so I should have just listened, without trying to advise you.

I wish you could be here to see Camelot, but if it's any consolation, my dad's making a video of it. I'm sure you'll understand if I say that I need to save all of my wishes for my mom right now.

Love, Ashley

I *did* understand that she needed all of her wishes for her mom, so I made a few of my own, on her behalf.

"Is Ashley okay?" Mireille asked later that evening. Between Conner and me, Mireille had heard so much about Ashley that she said she felt like they already knew each other.

"I think so," I said. "But her mom's in the hospital, so she's been worried."

"That would be very difficult," Mireille said, and sat down on my bed. "I'm lucky to have two parents – even though they are so strict!"

"They could be worse," I said. Mireille had been very

honest with me the night at the hotel, and now that I was no longer relying on chance to make decisions, I wanted to tell her about my father. "One of the reasons I don't want to e-mail my dad is that he was in jail," I said quietly, without looking up. "He was drunk-driving, and almost killed a child."

"That doesn't mean he is a bad person," Mireille reassured me with a hand on my shoulder. "He could have changed."

"Do you really think so?" I asked, ready to listen without prejudging her opinion, as she had taught me.

She nodded. "I know it. My mom used to spend all of our money at ... the casino," she looked away for a moment, as if remembering, before she continued. "But she stopped, just before Madeleine was born. And now she's good again."

Suddenly, I understood why Mireille had objected so vehemently to the card dealer outfits I'd suggested for the costume party. And what she'd meant at Halloween, about everyone having secrets.

"She *is* good," I said, thinking about how, right from the start, Sylvie had treated me like her own daughter, even if, or because, she was overly protective.

Mireille was thoughtful for a second before adding: "She didn't used to be so strict, before, but I think now she is more afraid that we will make bad mistakes, like she did. Still, there are some things we have to learn for ourselves."

* * *

On my last weekend with my host family, Sylvie and Gilbert suggested a trip out of town to a snow-tubing park. Even at Mireille's house, that second week of December, the snow was already halfway up the doorframe. Under Nicolas' guidance, I'd become an expert at shoveling. Tubing, he told me, would make me love the snow again, and turn me into "a true *Québécoise*."

There was joy on his face as he described the thrill of zipping at top speed down snow-covered hills on rubber inner tubes, and how he'd convinced his parents to take us all.

"*Tu vas?*" Mireille asked me, at the bottom of the first hill, likely remembering what a disaster I'd been at the circus school.

Admittedly, careening down runs so high that some of them boasted names like "Everest" and "Himalaya" would not have been my first choice of a family outing. And I *was* tempted to pull out my pendulum to make sure I wouldn't break my neck. But they were my family now, and I needed to trust them – and have faith in myself.

"*Oui. Je vais essayer*," I said, feeling myself go pale. "I'm going to try."

Nicolas grinned, and held his thumb and forefinger together to indicate something small. "*Petit?*"

"*Non*," I shook my head. If I was going to live my life, I wanted to do it wholeheartedly.

But not necessarily alone. I chose a large hill, with lots of twists and turns, and a tube built for six, so my new "sisters" and "brothers" could hold my hands.

The tube hurtled down the hill, with Mireille squealing and Madeleine squeezing my hand while the snow sprayed up cold on my face.

"*Fantastique?*" Sébastien asked, at the bottom.

"*Oui. Fantastique!*" I replied. I started up a bigger hill, knowing that it would take courage to make decisions when I couldn't predict how fast life would go, or what might be around the corner. But I was confident, now, that that was where I'd find the best surprises.

Chapter 18

Saying good-bye to Mireille was difficult, but I knew that we'd be together at my house, in just four weeks. Saying good-bye to her family was harder.

"*Retourne et visite encore!*" Madeleine and Sébastien demanded. I promised them I would, but knew that even if I did return, as requested, during spring break and summer holidays, everyone would be different. Marie-Claire would likely be off at college, and the little ones would inevitably be more grown-up and far less interested in their big sister's friend.

But then again, I thought, looking across the train station at the boy – no, *man* – who'd arrived only as my friend, sometimes change is good.

* * *

My own baby sister, Angelique, had also grown up a great deal while I'd been away. Now ten months old, she crawled everywhere, pulled herself up on furniture, and fell down all the time. Mom and Mike were used to it, but it was hard for me to watch her cry so much.

"She'll be okay," Mom reassured me. "*You* were doing the same thing once when your father visited, and he said that even if you never actually got anywhere, as long you kept getting up, you were already making him proud."

"Then it's too bad he didn't hang around long enough to see me at the circus school," I said, remembering my problems with the stilts.

Mom smiled sadly. "Oh, sweetie, why haven't you written him back?" she asked, brushing the hair out of my eyes.

"I don't know," I admitted. "I guess it just feels safer to not know why he left me than to ask him why, and find out that it was because he didn't love me enough."

* * *

The day after my arrival, I met Ashley at the mall for

Christmas shopping and catching up.

It was good to see her, but it turned out that she'd had a much rougher semester than she'd admitted to by phone or e-mail.

"It's been really hard to watch my mom be so sick," she admitted when I asked. "She pretty much ended up with every possible side effect you can get from chemo, and I couldn't really do anything to help, except reassure her that she'd make it through."

"That counts for a lot, though," I reminded her, thinking about the worst days, a year ago, right after Tyler's abuse. There'd been lots of times, back then, when I'd been unable to imagine ever being happy or confident again. It hadn't happened right away, or all at once, but eventually, I got over it. I wanted to believe that it would be like that for Ashley's mother too.

"What about all of the natural remedies you were looking into when I left?" I asked. "Didn't they help at all?"

"Most of that was disastrous, actually," she admitted.

Then I broached the subject of the rumors I'd inadvertently started about her on E-Me. A couple of people, she explained, had taken the gossip to the extreme, even after the pictures came down. That was why one guy had lost his role in the play, leaving Taiton to take the lead. "I still can't tell you how sorry I am about those comments ..." I said.

"It's okay," she said, sounding like she meant it.

"No. It's not ..."

"It was a *mistake*," she said. "There's a big difference between mistakes and malice. Mistakes are forgivable. Malice isn't."

"What's the difference?" I asked, wondering what categories Tyler and my father might fit into.

She thought about it for a minute. "Intent, I guess," she said. "Mistakes aren't things you do intentionally. And they're not things you tend to repeat. Like, your E-Me posting. You didn't intend it to be hurtful, and you also didn't do it again. It was a mistake."

It was so simple, and yet, when she said it, I had to steady myself against a wall and close my eyes.

I still didn't have enough information to categorize my father's actions as mistakes or malice. Tyler's abuse, on the other hand, was by her reasoning *unforgivable* – and always would be.

And because his actions were unforgivable, I didn't need to feel like a bad person for *not* forgiving him.

It was something I'd been told many, many times. And it was something I could say out loud, and almost believe.

But still, there had always, *always* been that lingering bit of doubt, like the faintest shadow of something I couldn't quite erase.

All year long, I'd sketched and painted, documenting my story, trying to heal. And all I'd really needed was a simple, almost mathematical formula. Malice equals unforgivable.

Which meant that finally, after all this time, I could forgive *myself*. Forgive myself for believing in a creep; for giving an undeserving jerk a second chance; for not protecting my heart; for being human.

Warmth and relief bubbled up inside me.

"You okay?" Ashley asked, touching my arm.

I was. For the first time in a long time, I was really okay.

"I think you just gave me the best present ever ..." I said, hugging her.

"Okay," she laughed, not knowing what I meant, but content to just let me be happy. "So what about everyone else on your list?"

I'd already begun an oil painting of Sylvie and Gilbert's home, but I wanted to buy things for the rest of the family. We continued to catch up while we shopped for Christmas presents for my host family. As I filled her in on everyone's personalities, she helped me choose the perfect presents for them too. I bought a henna tattoo kit for Mireille, who was adventurous and proud of her body. That way, she'd be able to adorn her skin in a more creative (and less permanent) way than the belly button ring she'd admired so much on me.

For Marie-Claire, who'd been like the big sister I'd always wanted, I bought a beautiful pair of satin pyjamas. I pictured her wearing them while she sat around with Mireille, talking, the way the three of us often had.

For Nicolas, who had begun drawing his own cartoons right after I'd arrived, I picked out a sketchbook and some new pencil crayons. And for Sébastien, who never stopped moving, a tiny karate outfit.

I wanted to get something lasting for Madeleine, as

now I felt like her honorary, older, English-speaking sister.

"I'm thinking about getting her a children's book," I said, as we finished up our shopping. "She really loves stories, and even though she speaks French," I said, scanning the display at the bookstore, "she adores practicing English with Mireille ..."

My voice faded away as my eyes fell upon a familiar title. It was a children's story and, once, I'd known it by heart. "I have my own copy of this book somewhere," I said to Ashley, turning it over in my hands, searching my memory for slippery recollections that I couldn't quite catch.

"I used to copy the drawings on this one page – right here ..." I showed her, then caught my breath sharply as I rediscovered the thing I'd most needed to remember, but had somehow forgotten. My eyes stung and my voice cracked as I read the words beneath the illustration:

I can't promise that you'll never have to be brave. But if you believe in yourself – as I already do – you'll find that all the strength you need is already inside of you.

"That's beautiful," Ashley breathed.

"This book came in the mail," I whispered, suddenly remembering the package that had arrived on my fifth birthday. "It came from my dad."

And as the memories resurfaced, it felt like a little part of me that had been sleeping had rolled over, kicked off the covers, and looked around for the first time.

Finally, I understood what everyone else had been trying to tell me about contacting my father. They hadn't been saying that I needed to *give him* a second chance. They'd been telling me that I needed to *take* one, *for myself.*

Chapter 19

*a*nd so, on a Sunday morning, I sat in front of my computer, and composed the following message:

Subject: From Caitlyn

Dear Scott (Dad),

Thank you for the birthday card. Sorry it took me so long to reply, but you've been out of my life for twelve years, so I didn't think you'd mind if I took some thinking time of my own before writing back.

I don't remember you very well, and to be honest, I was a little scared that I wouldn't live up to your expectations, or you to mine. I tried to find you on the Internet a couple of times over the years, but couldn't really figure out which Scott Collins among the very many you were until I had your address. Then I found an article about you having a DUI conviction, and I wasn't sure if I wanted to get to know you. I now realize that might have been unfair of me. But anyway, I thought you should know that I know, so you don't have to pretend or think you have anything to hide.

I would like to get to know you, now, if you are still interested. No promises on how I will feel once I do, but there really never are when you start a relationship.

Write back, or call.

Caitlyn

My throat was dry and my palms were sweaty by the time I added my phone number and hit the send button. I knew that British Columbia was in a different time zone, and that he might not access his e-mail immediately. But waiting for a reply was surprisingly difficult. For twelve years I'd heard nothing. For three months, I'd done nothing. And then, for four hours, I checked my inbox every ten minutes.

The telephone rang.

"Caitlyn?" a male voice said when I answered. It was familiar, like a song you know but haven't heard in awhile. "It's ... Scott. Your dad."

"Hi," I said.

"Hi," he cleared his throat. He continued, a bit hesitantly. "I, um, I wanted to thank you for your e-mail. For getting back to me. And for sending your number. Do you have some time right now to talk?"

I nodded, then, in the silence that followed, realized that wouldn't be enough over the telephone. Feeling as if I was back at the top of the first hill at the tubing park, I managed to squeak out a "yes."

There was a big sigh at the other end of the line, and I relaxed, knowing that he was just as nervous as me.

"Great," his voice grew stronger as he launched into a speech that he must have rehearsed many times. "I, uh, I wanted to let you know, right away, that I am beyond sorry for all of the years I've missed and the pain I've caused. I know I can't make that up to you, and I know you have every reason to have doubts about me now. I don't want to disrupt your life in any way. But I am in a place where I think I can become a positive, trustworthy, permanent part of your life. If you'll let me show you."

Could he really keep that kind of promise? Was it fair to expect him to? And how could I trust it to be different this time, if I didn't know exactly what had happened before?

"Maybe," I suggested in a voice that was barely above a whisper, "you could tell me a little bit about what happened, before. And ... and why I didn't hear from you for so long." Asking was a risk, but it was one I needed to take.

His voice broke. "There really is no good explanation," he said. "Except that I was stupid. I don't want to make excuses. There are none. But I *am* sorry."

Right away, I liked the way that he accepted responsibility, without excuses, and apologized. I watched my goldfish searching for food at the bottom of his tank as my dad continued telling me his story. "The article you found *was* about me. I was ashamed of myself, when I got arrested, so I didn't let your mother know."

"Then, I kept telling myself that I would contact you again as soon as I got myself together. But by the time that had happened, I knew I was going to be another disruption in your life ... and I began to think that you might be better off without me."

"I thought ... I thought *I* wasn't good enough for *you*," I choked. "I didn't *know* I thought that until a little while ago, but now ... I know that I did."

171

"Never, Caitlyn. It was never you," he reassured me, after so many years of me thinking otherwise. "You were the one good thing I'd done in my life. If you believe nothing else about me, please believe that."

For a moment, I considered all of the things I'd once believed – and recently discovered – about myself. I hadn't thought I was a risk-taker. But the risks I'd been taking had turned out pretty well. I hadn't thought I needed a father. But I'd envied Mireille because of hers, and I wanted to talk to this man, and get to know more about him, and about myself. And deep down, I hadn't thought that I deserved a second chance at happiness. *But I did.* And so did my father.

Our conversation went on for hours, and ended with the promise of additional phone calls, and a visit before the holidays were over.

* * *

Just before bed that night, I removed my belly ring. I'd been thinking about it for a long time, but especially since the night at the hotel, with Conner. When I'd looked down and seen it, I hadn't felt good or proud – I'd felt ashamed. The piercing would always remind me of the mistake I had made in trusting Tyler instead of myself. And even though some mistakes can't be undone, I didn't need to wear reminders of them on my body. Instead, I could carry them with me in my memory, as lessons learned.

I took off my turquoise mood ring, too, knowing that I still had questions, but that I had to look for the answers within myself.

Maybe I'll never find all the answers; maybe I have some now. And maybe sometimes the best answer is forgiveness.

Accolades & Awards for **Painting Caitlyn**

"Peters clearly has her finger on the pulse of teenage dating ..." – *School Library Journal*

"Realistic and powerful ... will stay with readers long after the book is closed." – *KLIATT*

"... more than just a simple problem novel." – *Booklist*

"... a provocative story with an important message." – *CM: Canadian Review of Materials*

Selected, International Reading Association "Young Adults' Choices" List

Selected, American Library Association "YALSA Quick Picks for Reluctant Young Adult Readers"

Winner, Elementary Teachers' Federation of Ontario Writer's Award, Women's Program

Shortlisted, B.C. Teen Readers' Choice Stellar Book Award

Selected by the Maine Coalition to End Domestic Violence for the "Knowledge is Power" Program

You've met Caitlyn ...
now hear her best friend's story:

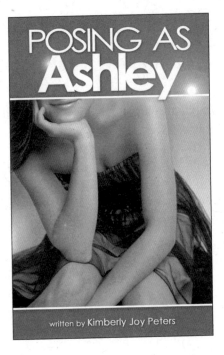

Posing as Ashley
by Kimberly Joy Peters / **978-1-897073-87-2**

Ashley seems to have everything going for her, but deep down she is plagued by self-doubt. Once she enters the hypercritical world of modeling, she is forced to make decisions that not only might disappoint those around her, but could also go against everything she believes in. Will Ashley chase what everyone else says she should want, or will she finally stand up for herself?

Accolades & Awards for **Posing as Ashley**

Get a sneak peek!

Turn the page to read the first chapter of
Posing as Ashley.

Chapter 1

$\mathcal{I}$ was the girl you wanted to hate. People joked about it, but I know it was true. They wanted to hate me because I was the girl they thought they couldn't be: the *smart* one, the *pretty* one, the *nice* one, the one with the *great boyfriend*.

Before I started modeling, that's what they saw, because that's all I showed them. The real stuff – the stuff inside – I kept hidden. I hid it because the imperfections that might have made me seem more human were the things that sometimes made me hate myself.

* * *

Though he caught the occasional glimpse of it, even my boyfriend, Brandon, didn't really know how much the deeper things, like my fear of never being good enough, shaped the outside Ashley that I portrayed to the rest of the world.

Brandon and I went out for almost two years. He has these amazing brown eyes and dark hair, but the thing I always liked best about him, right from the beginning, was that he was smart and that he wasn't intimidated by the fact that I always try to do my best at everything, too. All my life, kids have made snide comments about my academic abilities – I've been called names like "Brown Noser" and "Teacher's Pet" – which I never worried about, because I knew that most of it came out of jealousy. The part of me that's always doing my best is worth more than other people's jealousy, and Brandon got that, right from the start.

Even though he always said he loved the way I look – especially my long, thick dark hair – he was equally proud of the fact that I didn't try to coast by on my looks, pretending to be dumb, like a lot of other girls do.

Everyone thought we were the perfect couple. *I* thought we were the perfect couple. And I know that at one point, *he* believed it too. But at the beginning of the summer, Brandon changed his mind.

School had just ended for the year, and I'd thought we were going to hang out together – just the two of us – because he was leaving the next day to work at a canoe camp for the summer months. We'd planned to go to a movie, and I expected that it would be followed by a make-out session in his mom's car and a tearful goodbye with promises to write every day.

"Let's not go to the movie," he said when he picked me up. "Let's go sit out on the hill and talk."

I'd never seen him so serious, so I ran through possible "talking topics" in my mind, hoping maybe my suspicions were wrong. My mom had recently had surgery for breast cancer and I was scared for her, but Brandon and I talked about that all the time – he didn't need to make it a special issue.

I also wondered if it had anything to do with him going away – because he wouldn't have a cell phone or email access at camp – but we'd already been over that too. Neither one of us is insecure or jealous, and he'd actually said he was looking forward to getting real letters with lipstick kisses – letters that smelled like me.

Though it didn't make sense, I tried to prepare myself

for what I suspected might be coming next. We'd always had a great connection and had been able to tell each other anything, but we'd never started any conversations with "Let's talk." *Everyone* knows what that means.

"Okay," I said, reaching for his hand in the car. I thought I felt him jump just a bit when I touched him. "What's wrong?"

He glanced at me quickly, then down at our hands, before returning his gaze to the road and his hand to the wheel. "Your hands are all scratched," he said.

I didn't believe that that was the problem, but I explained: "We got a new litter of kittens at the animal shelter today, and they're at the perfect age for play-fighting."

"How many are there?" He seemed to relax slightly. I'd been volunteering at the shelter for five months and he liked hearing all about the animals.

"Six. Their mother is a little black cat named Raven, so I just slid one letter down in the alphabet and gave them all *s* names: Samson, Smokey, Sox, Sophie, Stella, and Sacha. Most of them are gray tabbies, but Samson and Sacha are black, like their mother."

Then I got quiet, wondering what Brandon really wanted to discuss, but I'm sure he just thought my mind was still back at the shelter.

"You'll find homes for them, Ash, even the all-black cats." He reached over and gave my hand a squeeze. As much as I always try to give off the impression of confidence in everything I do, I loved that he knew what I was worried about and that he wanted to comfort me. Black cats are the hardest ones to find homes for, even though some people consider them *good* luck and Julius Caesar is rumored to have kept one for that reason. I'd cried on Brandon's shoulder many times about the ones we couldn't place.

I'd always known I wanted to be a vet, and I hoped that someday when I was, I'd be able to offer low-cost clinics to spay and neuter people's pets. It was Brandon who'd suggested that to me – the idea of keeping the price down – when I'd started to get discouraged by the overflow of animals at the shelter. He often inspired me in that way, and I knew it was part of what I would miss the most while he was gone this summer.

We sat in silence during the rest of the drive to the

school and then walked together up a hill beside the field where I always sit to watch his football games.

"So?" I began.

"So, what?" he said, suddenly playing dumb. But I knew he had something on his mind.

"So what do we need to talk about?" I prodded, anxious to get things moving, regardless of which direction they were about to take.

"You. Us ..." his voice trailed off, and I swear I felt my heart breaking into a million pieces at that very moment. He went on to tell me all the things every girl wants to hear: how "amazing" I am; how I'm an "incredible combination of beauty, brains, and personality"; how "proud" he was to be my boyfriend; and how "great" the last couple of years had been.

When he'd finished the inventory of my good qualities, he started staring off into space, really intently. He wasn't looking at me, but at the goalposts out in the football field. It was as if he was being paid to watch them, should they become alive and try to make a break for it and escape out into the woods. I couldn't help but think that maybe he was wishing *he* could make a break for it and escape into the woods – because he knew what he was about to tell me, and he knew me well enough to know how I would react.

While he talked, I had such a sharp, excruciating pain deep down into my gut, that I thought for a second that there was something physically wrong with me. But then I realized that I wasn't breathing and that every part of my body was clenched tight.

"So are you actually going to come out and say it?" I finally asked in a small, measured voice that I almost didn't recognize as my own.

"Ashley – "

"You have to say it. You owe me that," I insisted, my voice hardly shaking, but my insides crawling now as if I was full of maggots. "You have to at least say it out loud."

"Ashley, you know I love you ..." he said. I could feel the biggest "but" of my life hesitating right there, on the edge of his lips, afraid to come out and meet me head-on.

"But I don't think we should be a couple anymore ... right now," he finished.

"So are you *dumping* me?" I asked without looking at him.

"No – I'm not dumping you. I still want to date you – sometimes – but I'm just saying that with me going away for the summer, we shouldn't be, you know, boyfriend/girlfriend anymore. We should both be free to see other people."

I felt as if I'd been tossed out of a moving car.

Ashley's story continues in:

Definitely NOT Camelot
by Kimberly Joy Peters / **978-1-897550-63-2**

It's only the first day of eleventh grade and Ashley is already generating a whole semester's worth of gossip. To add to the stress, her mother has started cancer treatments and Ashley's best friend, Caitlyn, is going on a foreign exchange trip, leaving Ashley to cope on her own. But Ashley, the consummate over-achiever, decides to face the school year head-on and tries out for the high school production of Camelot. Soon, she finds herself in a fairy-tale setting with a new love interest ... and a dangerous addiction.

www.lobsterpress.com

ABOUT THE AUTHOR:

Kimberly Joy Peters's debut novel, *Painting Caitlyn*, was published by Lobster Press in 2006, and has been recognized by the International Reading Association, the American Library Association, the Maine Coalition to End Domestic Violence, and the British Columbia Teen Readers' Choice "Stellar Book" Awards. Kimberly followed *Painting Caitlyn* with *Posing as Ashley*, a novel about Caitlyn's best friend. It went on to win the Elementary Teachers' Federation of Ontario Writer's Award and was selected for the Canadian Children's Book Centre's "Best Books for Kids & Teens." Kimberly teaches French and art in Beaverton, Ontario, a town near the shores of Lake Simcoe. Visit her at www.kimberlyjoypeters.com.

EMMA
Every Day

Party Problems

by C.L. Reid

illustrated by Elena Aiello

PICTURE WINDOW BOOKS
a capstone imprint

Emma Every Day is published by
Picture Window Books, an imprint of Capstone
1710 Roe Crest Drive, North Mankato, Minnesota 56003
www.capstonepub.com

Library of Congress Cataloging-in-Publication Data
Names: Reid, C.L., author. | Aiello, Elena, illustrator.
Title: Party problems / by C.L. Reid ; illustrated by Elena Aiello.
Description: North Mankato, MN : Picture Window Books, a Capstone imprint,
2020. | Series: Emma every day | Audience: Ages 5-7.

Summary: Eight-year-old Emma is excited about her best friend
Izzie's birthday party, but she is also a little worried because she
is deaf and communicates through sign language, and her
Cochlear Implant does not work well in noisy crowds.

Identifiers: LCCN 2020001371 (print) | LCCN 2020001372 (ebook) |
ISBN 9781515871804 (hardcover) | ISBN 9781515873112 (paperback) |
ISBN 9781515871880 (adobe pdf)

Subjects: LCSH: Deaf children—Juvenile fiction. | Birthday
parties—Juvenile fiction. | Best friends—Juvenile fiction. |
Cochlear Implants—Juvenile fiction. | CYAC: Deaf—Fiction. | People
with disabilities—Fiction. | Parties—Fiction. | Birthdays—Fiction. |
Best friends—Fiction. | Friendship—Fiction.

Classification: LCC PZ7.1.R4544 Par 2020 (print)
LCC PZ7.1.R4544 (ebook) | DDC [E]—dc23
LC record available at https://lccn.loc.gov/2020001371
LC ebook record available at https://lccn.loc.gov/2020001372

Image Credits: Capstone: Daniel Griffo, 28–29
Design Elements: Shutterstock: achii, Mari C, Mika Besfamilnaya

Designer: Tracy McCabe

Printed and bound in the United States.
PA117

TABLE OF CONTENTS

MEET EMMA

EMMA CARTER
Age: 8 Grade: 3

SIBLING
One brother, Jaden
(12 years old)

PARENTS
David and Lucy

BEST FRIEND
Izzie Jackson

PET
a goldfish named Ruby

favorite color: teal
favorite food: tacos
favorite school subject: writing
favorite sport: swimming
hobbies: reading, writing, biking, swimming

FINGERSPELLING GUIDE

MANUAL ALPHABET

Aa   Bb   Cc   Dd   Ee

Ff   Gg   Hh   Ii   Jj

MANUAL NUMBERS

0   1   2   3

Emma is Deaf. She uses American Sign Language (ASL) to communicate with her family. She also uses a Cochlear Implant (CI) to help her hear.

Kk   Ll   Mm   Nn   Oo

Pp   Qq   Rr   Ss   Tt   Uu

Vv   Ww   Xx   Yy   Zz

4   5   6   7   8   9   10

Chapter 1
Party Worries

Emma put on her Cochlear

Implant (CI) and spun in her

new dress. She was ready for

Izzie's birthday party. Izzie was

her best friend.

"Will everyone like this dress? Is it too fancy?" Emma asked Ruby.

Ruby was her goldfish. Emma loved talking to her.

"Do you think Izzie will like her gift?" Emma asked.

Emma had bought Izzie a pair of flippers. Her friend was crazy about mermaids.  Emma and Izzie loved to swim.

"I'm so nervous. Will I know anyone at the party? Will I understand what people are saying?" she asked Ruby.

Emma looked in the mirror one more time. "Wish me luck!"

Emma went to say goodbye to
Mom, Dad, and Jaden. Izzie lived
just a few houses away. Emma
could walk to the party by herself.

"I'm ready to go," she signed.

"Have fun," Dad signed.

"Bring me some cake," Jaden

signed. Emma laughed.

"Are you nervous?" Mom signed.

"A little bit," Emma signed.

"But I'm ready."

With one

final wave,

she walked

out the door.

Chapter 2
Party Time

Emma skipped all the way to
Izzie's house. When she rang the
doorbell, Izzie answered right away.

"Hello," Izzie signed.

Izzie knew sign language. She learned it when she met Emma two years ago.

"Happy birthday!" Emma signed, handing Izzie the present.

"I love your dress!" Izzie signed.

"Thank you!" One worry down.

Izzie's house was full of kids.

It was really loud. Emma looked

around. She didn't see anyone she

knew. She started to worry again.

Emma heard squeals and laughter, but she couldn't make out any words. Emma pressed a button and changed the program on her CI. Maybe that would help.

A girl ran over to Emma and pointed at herself.

"Sarah," she said as she fingerspelled her name. "I'm Izzie's cousin."

"Nice to meet you," Emma signed.

"Nice to meet you too," Sarah signed back.

Izzie ran over and grabbed
Emma's hand.

"Come on!" she said. "It's
time to go outside and play
the drop-the-bean-bag game."

In the backyard, the kids formed

a circle. They cupped their hands

behind their backs. Then they

waited.

Izzie would put a bean bag into

someone's hands, but whose?

The next second, the bean bag

fell into Emma's hands. She spun

around. Izzie ran past her. Emma

chased Izzie around the circle and

caught her arm.

"Ha! Ha!"

Izzie fingerspelled, laughing.

"You got me!"

Chapter 3
Mermaid Magic

After the game it was time
for cake. Everyone sang "Happy
Birthday." Emma sang and signed.
Izzie blew out the candles and
smiled. Everyone cheered!

The kids ran to the living room.

It was present time! Emma couldn't

wait for Izzie to open her gift.

She didn't have to wait long.

Izzie opened Emma's gift first.

"Cool!"  Izzie fingerspelled. "I love them! Let's go to the pool tomorrow. We will swim just like mermaids!"

"I can't wait!" Emma signed.

Izzie jumped up and swayed
like a mermaid dancing under
the sea. Everyone jumped up and
joined in the mermaid dance.

When the party was over, Izzie

gave Emma a huge hug.

"You really *mermaid* my day,"

Izzie signed.

"Well, we were *mermaid* for each

other," Emma signed back.

They both laughed and hugged again. Sarah came over and joined the hug.

Emma left the party with a new friend and no worries. She couldn't wait to tell Ruby all about it!

LEARN TO SIGN

friend

1. Lock fingers. 2. Repeat with other hand on top.

happy

Make two small
circles at chest.

birthday

Bring middle finger
from chin to chest.

cake

Make C shape and slide
down hand.

gift

Make X shapes and move
forward twice.

party

Make P shapes and
twist wrists.

thank you

Move hand away
from lips.

GLOSSARY

Cochlear Implant (also called CI)—a device that helps someone who is Deaf to hear; it is worn on the head just above the ear

deaf—being unable to hear

fingerspell—to make letters with your hands to spell out words; often used for names of people and places

flippers—flat, rubber attachments that are worn on the feet to help someone swim

nervous—feeling worried

overwhelmed—feeling too much of something all at once

relieved—free of pain or worry

sign—use hand gestures to communicate

sign language—a language in which hand gestures, along with facial expressions and body movements, are used instead of speech

TALK ABOUT IT

1. Emma likes to talk to her pet fish. Why do you think she does that?

2. Emma has a lot of worries before Izzie's party. Talk about a time you felt nervous. What did you do to feel better?

3. Use the fingerspelling guide at the beginning of the book to sign your name.

WRITE ABOUT IT

1. Make a list of things you can do to make yourself feel better when you feel nervous or overwhelmed.

2. Emma makes a new friend at Izzie's party. Write about a time you made a new friend.

3. Pretend you are Izzie. Write a thank-you note to Emma for the flippers.

Ruby

ABOUT THE AUTHOR

Deaf-blind since childhood, C.L. Reid received a Cochlear Implant (CI) as an adult to help her hear, and she uses American Sign Language (ASL) to communicate. She and her husband have three sons. Their middle son is also deaf-blind. Reid earned a master's degree in writing for children and young adults at Hamline University in St. Paul, Minnesota. Reid lives in Minnesota with her husband, two of their sons, and their cats.

ABOUT THE ILLUSTRATOR

Elena Aiello is an illustrator and character designer. After graduating as a marketing specialist, she decided to study art direction and CGI. Doing so, she discovered a passion for illustration and conceptual art. She works as a freelancer for various magazines and publishers. Elena loves video games and sushi and lives with her husband and her little pug, Gordon, in Milan, Italy.